BITTERS

a collection of GLBTQ vampire stories

by

Wendy Rathbone

The author weaves GLBTQ characters seamlessly into her stories and uses the vampire theme to poetically explore some hard questions about reality, identity, and love. (Two of the stories contain explicit m/m scenes.)

Unusual vampires people these pages. Orlando is a self-evolved vampire who does not realize how lonely he is until he meets the unique and enigmatic Carmel... Teror was born with an inability to feel emotion or empathy until he meets one of fourteen Aaron clones who have a special telepathic bond and they intend to extend it to him... Malachi is a vampire who feeds not on blood, but on light and love... Griffin is having an affair with a man he cannot see... One vampire lives in a mooncast shadow just beyond ordinary dreams... Jesse lives for lust and blood and does not believe in love, until one night that changes him forever... Charles and Barclay enjoy one last eclipse together...

Table of Contents

The Phantom on the Road

The girl ran from the limousine, tripping once on gilt high heels, then righting herself with a sob.

It was one of those nights when the sky and the land are the same color and you think you've fallen into a void. Not even the shadows could exist in this abyss, though I could have passed for one dressed in my dark vest and my silk black trousers. Always in black, I played the role. My vampire self was winning the battle I had begun long ago to become an outsider, no longer a man, but a never aging immortal.

The girl's hair was long, a rich dark gold. No one could have seen that clearly through this night had they not been like me, had they not been using preternatural vision. She was tall, and she wore a long, hip-hugging dress light in color, thin of material. Her arms were bare. She carried a clear plastic purse.

At first I thought the limo would wait for her return. I thought that the usual lover's quarrel could end with the girl getting back in the car, giving in.

Out here, we were away from the major part of the city. All that surrounded us were some little back roads, the highway and, about half a mile west, the sea. There were no houses, no hotels or buildings. I was walking here because I loved the silence. I had not been looking for excitement or entertainment. In fact, I'd been more or less meditating, and considering my options, which involved moving to the country for more peace, or going east where I'd heard most young vampires congregated to find like company. Of course, I'd have to leave my bodyguard job, and it was fun sometimes snarling at the fans of California celebrities who hired me.

Since I only worked at night, I earned more than the average guard. So I had money saved. And I had never been married to my career.

Anyway, to my surprise, the limo tires squealed, and it turned onto the highway, roaring down the black, empty road, leaving the girl behind.

She sobbed again, and gripped her arms tight to her stomach. The sob was angry but heartfelt, like a low moan. It was animal in tone, and my own stomach tightened in both empathy and wariness. Something wasn't right. As I looked at her, she appeared awkward, hurt, bent. And yet something else threw me, too, something I couldn't yet define. There was a terrible wrongness here, and I trusted my intuition and approached cautiously.

"Are you hurt?"

The girl whipped around. Her hair flew behind her in the dark, a shiny cape. I saw her face then, bruised at the eyes, bleeding at the lips. Her arms were scratched as well. Obviously more than a lover's quarrel.

"I—I—" She tried to speak. Her throat worked hard, swallowing tears, voice deep with pain.

"Can I help you?"

The eyes were blue, like sapphires in my night vision. The gaze was very hurt, very frightened. She looked away quickly as if hiding something, and shook her head.

"It's a long way from the city."

"Where am I?" A shy whisper.

"Out on highway 43."

"Do you have a car?"

"I was just walking."

The eyes glittered behind what I could now see were false eyelashes. She looked so young. It was almost as if she were in costume.

"It's okay," she rasped, turning away.

"You look like you need help."

Her head shook. She took a step away from me.

6

"Will he be back?" I asked, thinking the limo might be returning.

"Please, just leave me alone."

The tone made me frown. But when she stumbled again and fell to her knees, I was at her side in an instant. I couldn't just leave her.

Humans were like phantoms to me, busy ants rushing through their lives to satisfy hive-like whims. Their lives within their confines were complex series of dramas and emotion, pain, pleasure, grief, anger. But the outsider I had become had come to see it all as so unreal, like a story of fiction that gives an initial jolt of pleasure or sadness, then ends. It does not move on. It does not become more than it is.

So the phantoms populated the streets and the buildings, the phantoms ruled, yes, and I did not feel a part of that, but I also was not without compassion for them. I was detached, but still gentle with them, apart but not without human tenderness. I was a young vampire learning to live in my own world, but I had not sacrificed my heart to get there.

I lifted her by her shoulders. Her bare arms were smooth, thin, and hard muscles under the skin contracted. Veins stood out on her forehands as she twitched, half-awake, but still dazed. I brought her closer to me. I could smell jasmine perfume, but beneath that something else. Blood from her scratches. Alcohol on her breath. And more, a scent that she was not what she pretended to be.

I am clever and the clues were all there. But her face was so beautiful, so young, that for a moment I denied what I knew. A tear fell from her eye and down her bruise-dark cheek to her temple, nesting in soft, bronze hair. Her mouth opened to gasp in air. I touched her chin. I didn't need to go further. Embarrass her. Or myself.

The shadow of stubble gave it away.

I held a boy in my arms. I don't think he was more than about seventeen.

When the blue eyes opened, I asked, "Where does it hurt?"

"He beat me. It was the worst time." More tears fell. "'You are too old now,' he said. 'Too old.'" The voice cracked. It was a man's voice with a cadence that could pass for a deep female tone.

"This person who beat you—is he your father?"

Eyelashes fluttered. Blue powder on the lids glimmering. "Father?" He took a breath, rouged lips trembling. "No. Not my father."

"Do you have a home?"

"I knew no one but him for the past eight years. When I was nine I went to live with him."

"You need a hospital."

"No!"

"What is your name?"

"Carmel. Like the sauce." He tried to sit up. "It's because of my hair."

It was indeed the color of caramel, and longer than even mine, curling down below his waist. "Can you walk, then?" I asked.

He tried to stand. I could see the stains on the dress now, red and muddy. He was in bad shape. I was afraid he could've been internally injured.

I caught him when he fell again. He did not come to this time, and so I easily lifted him into my arms and started the long walk back toward the city. I was glad for my inhuman strength, for he was slim but not light. He was medium-tall in height for a male, maybe five-ten or eleven, and I could feel the muscles of his thighs against my arms, firm and strong, if lean.

His hair brushed my legs as I walked. For more than an hour I carried him without detection by other humans, and without rest. I thought about the hospital. I thought about how frightened he'd been at the suggestion of one and decided that I could take him home with me. I was not without skills at healing. I had a shaman's soul, a witch's hands.

The dark of the room enfolded the bed, and him. Only a little light from outside, a dull sodium streetlight through damask curtains, cast any glow on his body.

I did not turn on the lamp. I could see what had to be done. I cleaned him thoroughly, laid him naked on the cool sheets and began bandaging the broken ribs, the cuts on his arms and thighs. He did not awaken.

I listened to his breathing, his heart, and assessed that his loss of consciousness was not coma, but more an escape from pain, a weariness at such a hard life.

When I finished, I smoothed his long hair back from his face and tied it with a rubber band. I think I fell in love with him then, my stomach flipping, everything—the room, the bed, the floor—tumbling and tilting at the powerful awareness of emotion, like a punch of reality from another realm smacking me in my own self-imposed quiet, my silence.

I covered him. Without the evidence of his body, his face could easily have passed for a girl's. He was that soft-featured. That sweet. Sometimes the beautiful ones did not have it easier. They met dark fates because they were alluring, and because others treated them as objects, as dolls, as fantasies no more real than a dream.

So I had to ask myself, was I falling into the same trap? Had he mesmerized me from the moment he'd stumbled from the black limousine? Was beauty, after all my humbling lessons about the world of human phantoms and petty dramas, still strong enough to lure me back to the shadowland of mortals?

I took a deep breath, trying to regain my senses. Of course I could feel love, but with mortals it was dangerous. They could coerce, through the guise of love, the immortal back into the daylight, back into living the human plays and dramas as if *they* were eternal. A vampire could forget himself and regress. I was looking for someone of my own kind. It was why I'd been contemplating moving. I didn't want to love ephemeral things, and those I did love would surely break my heart. For becoming a vampire was not as easy as myth would decree it. It took a transformation of the mind as well as the body. Not just anybody had the stamina. And my own journey had taken well over twenty years. I did not transcend the human world by merely drinking blood or meditating or memorizing the higher truths of Anne Rice and Carlos Castaneda.

I decided then that I would help Carmel, but I would have to send him away when he was well.

I heard the door to the guest room open. He came into the living room where I sat reading by fire and candlelight. I must have looked strange to him, lounging on the couch with my feet up, my long dark hair streaming over the pillows, my candles flickering from all models of holders: skulls, gargoyles, fairies, demons, crystals, pumpkins, red glass jars.

Like I said, I played the part. I was still learning about that, that the part and the being were not the same, that I could be myself and not necessarily have to dress in velvet, and light black tapers, and covet capes. Yet I liked that world, the Gothic strain, the inky eyeliner and the satin vests and the big rings on long-nailed hands. I liked to think I lived permanently in Halloween; the poet in me craved all things of night and autumn. I'd been writing verse in dust since I was eleven years old.

He wore a dark velvet robe I'd left for him, and though he wasn't short, as I said, it dwarfed him. I am taller and bigger, and it had fit me perfectly.

He stood, like a hunched, overgrown child, and stared with his deep blue eyes.

I rose. It had been almost a full day that he slept. "Would you like something to eat?"

He ignored the question, squinting, then frowning. "Where are my clothes?"

"I've sent them out to be cleaned. The dress might not be saved, they said."

Now he would not look at me.

"I'm sorry. Maybe I shouldn't have done that—"

He shook his head once, then moved slowly, painfully, toward a buffet where I had half a dozen candles. He stared at them, hands nervously clenched in the pockets of the robe.

"I have aspirin if you're in pain," I offered.

He did not respond.

"Carmel," I said, "is that your real name?"

"It is now," he said quietly.

"Mine's Jonathon, but it's so ordinary that I often tell people my name is Sterling, or Rupert, or Orlando."

"Which do you prefer?" He still would not look at me.

I laughed. "It's Orlando for now."

Now he turned. "Thank you, Orlando." I saw his face darken and realized he was blushing. "Long ago, I was Mark. I hate that name."

"Do you like Carmel?"

He shrugged. I saw he was shaking.

"Why don't you sit. I have bread and cheese. Would you like a sandwich?"

He shrugged again, but he came and sat down, wincing from obvious pain in his ribs. He folded the robe tightly about his knees, then crossed his legs daintily. It was natural for him, not affected, or self-conscious. It was why I had not immediately known him for a boy in a dress.

I went into the kitchen and fixed a plate. I ate human food on occasion, which was why I kept it in the house; I ate when I was bored or really craving a taste, but I no longer depended on food for energy and sustenance. I did not belong to that process anymore, though I was still new enough at this

11

different life to find myself wanting it, like a person who kicks a smoking habit but still craves that rare cigarette. As a vampire, the blood kept me mostly satisfied, and was not difficult to obtain. My donors were unaware because I tapped them outside their reality. They could not comprehend it, and I cannot explain it better than that, but I had what I wanted without ever being caught.

Carmel ate the sandwich and drank the juice I brought him. His hair was still tied back. It fell in waves down his back as he bent to clean his plate. He was quite lovely and again I found myself taken in by him.

"You're welcome to stay until you get well," I told him.

He looked up. "You confuse me."

"What?"

"I thought you'd be mad."

"About what?"

He frowned and put the plate on my mahogany coffee table. "About me. About how I look, how I was dressed..." He let the sentence trail.

"Did you think I would treat you differently because you weren't a girl?"

"Well, yes." His eyes brightened with sudden tears.

I had no words then. I simply shook my head. Such a beautiful world I had left. And such a cruel one, too.

Soon after he ate he went back to bed. I made sure he was asleep before I left to hunt.

I could only think of Carmel as I drank from the young woman's wrist. She slept as I took her blood, and dreamt erotic dreams. I left her sweaty and a little paler, but happier than she'd been.

When I checked on him it was almost four in the morning. The covers were pushed to his waist. He was turned slightly on one side, facing the doorway, and his long pony tail snaked over his arm to pool on the sheet by his stomach.

As I started to turn away, he moaned. I noticed then that his face was damp, his hairline soaked. I moved forward and put my hand on his forehead.

The fever was like a fire on his damp skin. He did not awaken, even when I came back with water-soaked towels and wrapped him, or when I decided to move him to a tub of cold water.

After about fifteen minutes in the water, he started to come around. First he fought me. His bruised body flailed. He cried out nonsense, the name Frances, then moaned. He pushed at my hands and chest, muttered, "No no no," then began to cry.

I brought him out of the water and bundled him in the warm, velvet robe after doing my best to re-bandage his wounds, then carried him back to the bed. He clung to me. He begged forgiveness. For what I do not know.

I held him until the sun came up.

Then I left him quietly sleeping and went into my own, dark room.

That evening I found him sitting on the couch. The television was turned on to low volume, a sitcom of one sort or another, one I did not recognize.

He did not acknowledge me for a good five minutes. I sat beside him, waiting. Finally, I reached out to touch his face. He flinched. I ignored it.

"Good. Your fever is gone," I commented.

After a while he sat up straighter, the legs crossing, his long fingers folding and unfolding in his lap. He clicked the mute button on the remote, and turned to stare at me. "I had a dream last night that you attacked me."

"You were feverish."

"I ate some more of your food," he said.

"Good."

Now he frowned, staring at me more intently. "You are very strange. You don't seem bothered at all."

"About what?"

"Me being here. Me being so sick last night."

"Well, if you felt I attacked you—" I began.

"That was just a dream. But I woke up later. You were holding me. You were in the bed with me."

"I'm glad your fever passed."

"Are you gay?" he finally blurted.

I smiled. "Are you?"

"Well...yeah. Of course. I mean—" He looked flustered. His long hair was tied back up in the rubber band neatly; he must have found my combs, my shaving kit.

"Carmel," I said. I leaned closer to him. I smelled my own spice soaps on his skin, in his hair. He must have taken a shower as well. "I'm not like you."

"I'm sorry," he began.

"No," I interrupted. "I mean certain words and labels don't move me, don't concern me. I don't see the way you do. I don't have the same understanding of this world."

"I don't follow." His blue eyes grew serious. They were vibrant. I was pleased to see he was not a stupid boy.

"I mean I still have feelings like you. I look like you. I wanted to help you. But I'm not like you."

"You're not gay."

I shook my head. "I don't subscribe to labels. What are you asking," I said, flipping the question. "Do you want my personal sexual history?"

His head tilted. "You are strange."

For a moment, I felt bereft. Alone. I'd chosen my own destiny. But sitting here with him was difficult, because I couldn't really communicate myself, couldn't really have him know me. As a vampire, and as an immortal, anything between us, even the unusual pull in my gut that drew me toward him, was an amalgamation of chemical and illusory response. It was real but not what it wanted to be, or

14

pretended to be. I wanted to really share myself, but I couldn't. I could love him, but never have that love that I craved, that embrace of knowing. I didn't even think that kind of relationship could exist with other vampires, but at least they wouldn't grow old and die.

I gazed at him. I reached out my hand to his face and this time he didn't flinch. "Do you want my personal history?" I asked again. He was so very beautiful. My stomach turned into a knot.

"I didn't mean…I want…I'm sorry," he stuttered.

"It's all right."

"Everything I do is—" He hesitated. "It's bad. It's wrong." He bowed his head. The sobs came, then.

"Like what?" I asked calmly. I let my hand rest on his shoulder.

His hands balled into fists, clutching the thick robe. The words came out forced, angry. "Like everything! Me. My age. How I look. The dresses. The guys. He beat me because of it. I thought he liked me like a girl. He did. I know he did. But then he hated me, called me names because I got older, got bigger. I don't know how else to be. Since I was five I was secretly wearing dresses. I thought he liked me for that and more. But when I started to grow hair, you know, on my body, he stopped liking me. Do you know how old I am?" He looked up. I didn't say anything. "I'm seventeen. And I've been raped and beaten more times than I can count. Because I'm so wrong. Because I deserve it."

"Why didn't you just leave?"

"I didn't have a key."

"What do you mean? He kept you locked up?"

He shrugged. "I sold myself to him, you know. I thought it was what I wanted."

"At nine you thought that was what you wanted?"

Again, he shrugged. "You don't understand." The tears returned. "I liked it." He became very shy, perhaps even ashamed, and would not look at me. "I did. Sometimes. When he was nice to me. When it was fun and games. Is that bad? I wouldn't blame you if you were completely disgusted."

I shook my head. "Why would I be disgusted? It's not bad until you want someone to stop the game and they don't."

"Yeah. I guess it was like that." But he seemed unsure. Insecure.

"Did you love him?"

He wiped his eyes on the back of his hand. "He told me I was beautiful. That was all I wanted." The words were dead inside him, toneless.

We sat in silence for a long time. I could feel that he'd shut me out. He was ashamed, embarrassed, confused. I could tell he wanted to be alone. Finally, I patted him on the shoulder and rose. "I have to go out for a while. Will you be okay?"

He nodded, and turned the sound to the TV back on.

When I came home, he was asleep again, curled on the couch like the kid he was.

I went to my room and read for a while, then dozed into the early, pre-dawn hours.

Soft footsteps on carpet woke me. My door was open. He stood looking into my room, eyes so sad, head tilted down.

I sat up on my bed. "Carmel? What's wrong?"

"I don't have anywhere to go. I don't feel real, Orlando."

My heart pounded. I wanted to hold him again. But the danger of regression assaulted me. I was still so young myself, barely twenty as a vampire, seventy-seven in total years. I could not get caught up in a young man's life. In the mortal world. In that fleeting play again. I had worked hard for my immortality, my gifts and my talents. I was afraid that if I loved him and he couldn't see the real me, I would stop being me for a while, and forget my vampire ways. I didn't want that.

16

And yet I felt myself respond to him.

I had never answered his question the night before about my personal sexual history. I had loved. But only fully as a mortal. Never as a vampire. And men, well, they were conquests I had experienced, but I had only ever fallen in love with women. Ninety percent of the time, women were my donors.

I got up. As I approached him, he backed up a step. But I reached out and touched his shoulders, then pulled him to me. "You're not real, Carmel. That's why you feel this pain. No one has ever let you just be yourself. You've only been what others wanted, an object to mold." I held him then, feeling his warmth, his tension, his pain. After a moment, he relaxed and I felt his arms lift at my waist.

"Do you understand what I just said?" I asked.

"I don't know how else to be." I felt him embrace me tighter. His body pressed to mine.

I stepped back. It wasn't that I didn't want him. But he was too needful right now.

"Are you going to throw me out?" he asked suddenly, bowing his head.

When I didn't answer right away, he backed up a step. His hands came together at his waist and I reached for them. "No," I said. "No."

Now he met my eyes. "Why not?"

"Maybe I can help you. I don't know. But I think I want to try."

Carmel recuperated very quickly. Soon, even the pain in his ribs faded, for he could sit now without wincing.

He came into my room one night just as I was getting ready to go out. I had a job for a few hours at a concert. I hoped I would find a donor there as well.

"You like all this dark stuff, don't you?" He was looking at a picture on my wall, of angels with black wings and sharp teeth.

"I do."

"All your candles, and the black clothes and hair. You work at night. You live like a vampire."

"Well, what do you think about it?"

"It's cool, I guess. The Goth scene. But it seems, well, depressing. I don't mean that as a judgment or anything," he added quickly.

"Is that how you see me?"

"Not really."

"Have you ever wondered how I got you here that first night? I didn't have a car. I carried you. It was over twenty miles."

He frowned.

"You were severely injured. I healed you." I looked down at my palms. How they had flamed when I'd put my hands on him. "You should have gone to a hospital in your condition."

"What are you saying?"

"Didn't you ever wonder? Don't you think about things like that? Things that just don't fit with this world?"

"All the time." He smiled. It was lovely.

"You said the other day you felt unreal. Do you even know what is real and what isn't?"

He laughed at first, quietly, softly. It was not ridicule. He'd been ridiculed enough in his life to know how it felt. He did not have any of that kind of cruelness within him, no matter how much it had been heaped on him.

"Are you saying you're a real vampire?"

To answer was not a simple process. I had worked hard to mentally transcend Carmel's world, yet I still lived within it. I had suffered to learn to see the way reality wheels and turns, how it is so connected to thought and belief, how it is so very very fragile when you turn to look at it from odd angles and when you can move outside it and yourself and see time as a box with a closed lid. Of course, inside that box were precious things, jewels, but with them came the price of mortality, of time. Carmel was in the box. He was a diamond shining in my eyes. How could I take it and not be pulled back in?

My vision blurred.

"I'm sorry," he said suddenly. The emotion on my face must have alarmed him. He came to me. He sat beside me and put his arms around me, his head on my shoulder. "Maybe you don't think I understand, but I do. I can tell you that when I put on the dresses and the make up, I feel lighter, like I'm in a good dream I never want to let go. It isn't what people think, like it's bad or about perversions, it's about taking away the veils of this world."

As he spoke, his words amazed me.

"All of it is like a dream, but for me it's been mostly a bad one. I can't always say why. It's like I feel strange and wrong. I knew I was gay when I was very little. It upset people also to see me play with dolls, or want to play more with girls instead of football with the boys. When they became upset, it was as if they thought I could just stop being who I was, I could just change because that was the rule, that was how I should be, like a good boy, and never go outside the lines. There were some people who were harsh and judgmental, and some who weren't, but the consensus, whether they were being loving or gentle, or whether they were cruel, was that I was an embarrassment, that I would never be happy in their world…their world that wouldn't accept me.

"Now, even in my strangeness, you accept me. I like dresses. They make me feel free, real. It doesn't bother you."

I shook my head. "No. It really doesn't."

"But you're not like me, so how can that be?"

"I've told you—"

"I know. I remember. You said you don't have the same understanding of this world that it demands, that labels don't concern you. But you also think I can't accept you. You think that you are even further away from this world than a guy who wears a girl's clothes. You think I wouldn't be able to believe in you, to affirm you, to see you."

"Something like that." I leaned back. He was staring at me, open, innocent. What was this creature?

"But I can see you. Just like you can see me. Maybe I can't see all of you. Maybe I think you are very very different, for rescuing me for one thing, and not kicking me out of your house for another. But I want to see all of you. I want to try. To learn."

"I can only go forward," I said.

"What do you mean?"

"I am immortal."

He didn't flinch.

"And," I continued, "I would only ever, always leave you behind."

Now his eyes grew clouded. "But couldn't you try to take me with you?"

I cupped his face with my hands. I had heard of catalysts, a rare condition of our kind where we could inspire another to evolve. Most vampires were unable to teach their true wisdom to mortals. Humans were not receptive. Most vampires couldn't even do the transfusions required in the final step of transforming the physical body to withstand eternity. They were too weak, or too selfish with their own energy, needing it for their own survival. It had been my own will in the end which had transformed. This evolution was not something that could be done for another.

But when I looked at Carmel, I knew I would have to try. I wouldn't leave him behind if I could help it, and I would help him prepare himself for this if, in the end, he chose to stay with me.

I had been thinking of moving to look for other vampires. To find companionship for my silence, my nights.

But companionship had found me, strangely. I was not unused to synchronicities such as these. In fact, I paid close attention to them.

In answer to Carmel's question, I leaned forward, and placed my lips on his, drawing him to me.

It was as if the phantom had just become real.

The Boy Without a Soul

Elizabeth was a cold town cuddled in northern pines that gave little shelter, so it came as no surprise that it could spawn such a mechanism as Terrance Butro. He grew up as Teror, though he did not earn the name until his later years, and some said the name was unfair even then.

Teror's father worked as a logger. In his spare time, he switched to 'drunk', dying young at thirty-eight. For his son, he showed no concern or patience. He was a man of damaged psyche, as forgotten by the world as all victims of life eventually are. He lived for the sounds of saws, the scent of wood dust, the tranquilized stupor of cheap ale. Teror remembered him as one remembers a vaguely interesting mannequin in a storefront window. The father rarely moved, and the eyes held only distance and plastic regret.

Teror's mother never had the chance to discover her own psyche, let alone translate her husband's, or her child's. Married at seventeen, she lived confused by the expectations of the males in her family. She loved Teror in her way, kept him groomed, fed, made sure he attended school, but he was a difficult boy to like, and other kinds of love which she longed to give him became bottled up inside her to form a hollow ache. For Teror was not a hugging child, nor could he be kissed without some expression of displeasure wrinkling his face. As an infant, he'd cry emptily if rocked or coddled. After the age of two, he never cried again. Nor did he ever learn to smile.

If you were to watch a medley of scenes chosen from among Teror's school years, you would see a tortured child, an isolated boy, a quiet blond kid with a poker face—heart-shaped lips in a pale portrait, eyes like splotches of ink on snow—and decide at once that he was too beautiful to ignore, and that your special knowledge of love would constitute the miraculous formula to cure him.

In truth, Teror cared about nothing. It was therefore impossible for him to be unhappy. Far from tortured, events might be seen by him as ineffectual.

Second grade: Little Molly Florbanks falls during ice skating into a frozen pool. She screams. Her heavy woolen coat acts as a sponge, adding dozens of pounds to her flailing form. Teror sees it all, his calm, big eyes unmoving as Molly churns and cries. If he notices anything, if he has a reaction at all, it is to the way light plays off the ice in Molly's brown hair, giving her a cap of silver—the winter sun captured in diamonds of frost. He is neither glad nor sad to see this. Simply mesmerized, then uninterested as older kids come to her rescue.

Fifth grade: Teror falls from the top of a playground slide, landing in frozen sand, one arm trapped beneath him. As he picks himself up, his arm is bent in the wrong place. Between wrist and elbow, the skin tents in two places. Classmates gasp. The teacher sends someone off to call the nurse, makes him stay quiet, keeps asking how he feels. Teror stares at his arm in the same way he stared at Molly's hair. The arm throbs a little, but feels like someone else's limb, bone, skin. Pain is just another thing to experience for Teror, like eating, or learning arithmetic. He is not special. It certainly doesn't touch anything deep within him. Nothing does, though he knows at this point in his life that others experience another way. That something called longing, need, want, hate, even love seems to drive people, and that empathy—a word he's looked up in the dictionary so many times the page is torn and frayed—gives people an instant understanding of others that Teror has never known.

Eleventh grade: It seem all boy-talk, when not in the company of girls and adults, is about sex. Teror's curiosity precludes normal excitement. Tab A in slot B with other variations. It mesmerizes him only long enough for him to discover how babies form. Then it's on to another math problem, or a reading assignment involving what to Teror are useless philosophies. And yet the sex talk is continuous, a part of the social structure, a part of growing up. Teror listens. Teror searches himself for any reaction that might match the other boys. They all talk of girls, of what they do or want to do to them. A couple, he notices, eye boys with a certain similar enthusiasm. They are either the loudest advocates for girl-jumping, or the quiet ones shying away on the edge. But none are as quiet as Teror. And he sees no difference between girls and boys, and certainly no preference. So one afternoon when the loudest advocate throws the quietest one on the shower room floor and spreads his legs, Teror thinks that maybe this will be the time he feels something. This will be when the border separating Teror from anger and fear and desire and hate and joy will be tunneled, will be crossed. The loudest one scrapes into Teror, grunting, breathing hard sour breath into his face. There is pain which is as uninteresting as nothing, neither filling him nor emptying. Other things are done to him. Teror is left on the shower tile with blood and semen sprinkling his thighs. Another boy with a perpetually alarmed expression on his face helps him to his feet. Teror doesn't understand why he bothers.

It was only after Teror graduated high school and left Elizabeth that he found a way around his problem.

The story actually began with Aaron Endicott, who was a famous dead singer with a myth of immortality surrounding him much like the myths of Valentino, Elvis, Marilyn Monroe, and Michael Jackson. He died young of alcoholism, but was rich and eccentric enough to have his body preserved by the Alcor cryonics laboratories in the hopes of being revived some day. Because of that, it seemed to the world he'd never really died. People reported seeing him at various places such as Burger King, Disneyworld, or corner pubs in just about every town in the world. But one day he really did live on in a number of illegally cloned bodies, all of whom resembled the superstar in physical stature—shimmering blue eyes, thick black hair—but nothing more.

The Aaron clones were a test of some mad but ingenious fan who worked at Alcor and was later imprisoned for criminal genetic experimentation. They grew up in various foster or adopted homes, fourteen of them, and were as famous as their progenitor twin if for no other reason than the both disturbing and delightful fact that Aaron lived again. But as they grew, it became apparent they were unique in a capacity aside from the genetic make up. All fourteen had a kind of psychic link. When one was hurt, the others instantly knew it. There were even tests given to some of the boys that seemed to prove a rudimentary telepathy existed between them. All fourteen boys—Baron, Caron, Deron, Eron, Feran, Garon, Harrin, Jaron, Kieran, Loren, Merlin, Nerin, Oren, Perrin—had a natural ability to put others at ease, to calm a crowd, to lead it. Some people even claimed one touch from an Aaron clone and you'd be healed of whatever afflicted you.

The boys were deemed to be too young for such pressures and were hidden far apart from each other to grow up as normal as possible. They kept in touch, and each one grew up into an independent, intelligent young man—although not a one developed any interest in music. Six of them opted for college educations.

And that was how Harrin, known also as Harry, came to be in the same city as Teror, and how being men in pursuit of great experiences, yet too young to be taken seriously, they both enrolled in the university.

Suspicion reigned right away in the college dorms that Harry was one of the Aaron clones, despite Harry's attempts to act, speak and wear his hair differently from his progenitor's. That he was Teror's roommate meant Teror also got a certain amount of unwanted attention. But because Teror was so calm, because Teror didn't seem concerned, that nonchalance rubbed off and soon the rumors became yesterday's excitement—about as interesting as a Teflon skirt or who won for World Governor in '26.

Teror saw Harry as nothing more or less than a roommate, so when Harry thanked him for being such a good guy and not making a big deal over the fact that he was a clone, Teror said, "Is it a big deal?"

"To most people, yes," Harry said.

Teror watched the usual coming together of the eyebrows, the narrowing of the mouth, the general contorted look of those who tried to fathom him when he made what to them were inept comments. "Most people," Teror echoed. "Oh." Then went to his desk, turned on the light, and waved on his computer.

Their conversations were nearly always that short, and Harry seemed to naturally understand and accept that Teror preferred a good word or number game on the computer over gossip, or any verbal discussion for that matter. It occurred to Teror that he could've thanked Harry for his understanding in return, but then he decided there was no point. He didn't care if Harry was understanding or not. Besides, Harry had misinterpreted Teror's lack of concern over his clone status for being a decent human being. And Teror had never felt decent or human.

Despite short conversations and both boys' eccentricities, Teror and Harry got along well. They kept to similar schedules, even shared a couple of the same classes. Teror's talents excelled in the area of mathematics, while Harry transcended the humanities. They learned to work together for optimum benefit.

Teror had never lived so close to another human being before. Not his mother, not anyone. He was able to observe behavior he hadn't ever noticed in schoolmates. For example, just before Harry went to bed, he got a faraway look in his eyes and nearly stopped breathing. Teror had heard of epilepsy and wondered if this were some kind of seizure. Finally, curiosity prompted him to ask.

"What is that you're doing?"

The small room—white brick walls, brown carpet— housed two beds, two desks and two dressers. There was barely enough room between the necessary furniture for a walkable path. Their desks sat side by side against the dormer window. As Teror swiveled his chair, they were face to face, knees nearly touching. The bright lights over the desk computers threw the rest of the room in uneven shadow.

"Communicating," Harry answered.

"Communicating?"

Harry nodded once, his soft eyes distracted, unfocused. "With my brothers."

"I don't understand." It was common for Teror. So much about human behavior eluded him that he rarely voiced his confusion anymore, finding it easier to just let the passion and intensity of others rush by him untapped, never conceived.

"I know you don't understand. You miss a lot by being the way you are. I've been discussing you with some of my brothers. We've been forming theories."

"You talk to them? In your mind?"

Harry's hair flopped forward as he nodded. He kept it long, slung in a ponytail, but by evening it hung loose and dark, only the longest ends still caught in the black ribbon he used.

"Can you hear each others' thoughts all the time?" Teror asked. Curiosity was the only thing he'd ever felt that came close to true emotion. Though the intensity of that was purely intellectual, it caused his metabolism to slightly elevate.

"Thoughts and feelings," Harry replied. "But not all the time. During a trauma, or when we trance-out."

"Is that what you do every night? Trance-out?"

"Yes, with my brothers in this time zone. The others are further away, so it's harder. But we all stay in touch."

"It's because you're clones," Teror said quietly, now staring out the window at the golden campus lights. They were like a sea of dimmed or dying stars.

Teror faced Harry again. "What theories?"

"In time." His voice came soft, almost multi-toned. It was as if more than one Harry spoke those two words. An echoed Harry.

Teror would wait. He didn't care if 'in time' meant forever. Nothing would change.

Something about Harry drew people to him. It wasn't just his famous looks and origin—he was gentle, open, caring. He laughed at all the right times, gave a sympathetic presence when required, never seemed to have a down mood or bad day. When it rained, he glowed. During thunderstorms, his life-force, a palpable entity people swore they could actually feel emanating off him, grew brighter, stronger.

Teror noticed all of this, living in such close confines with the renowned clone, but still felt nothing within his own make up that might draw him to Harry the way others were. Harry was his roommate, nothing more. He could see that Harry moved through a kind of magnetic field of power, of vitality. There was almost a rainbow effect about him, light glancing off dark hair in blues, in silver, gold skin shifting with the shadows that threatened to mar it, blue eyes sparking from some depth of being that mystified Teror even more. The high forehead, the square-ish face, even the somewhat sad set of eyes never seemed to interfere with the feeling that Harry was always smiling. He never drank. He never did drugs. "I have a low tolerance for chemical substances," he'd tell people. "It'd be too easy for me to abuse the privilege." It seemed, though, that Harry didn't need to drink or get high to join in a party atmosphere. He fit in everywhere. He brought to life the very air around him wherever he went.

"Okay," Harry said to Teror one quiet night when the rain made everyone sleepy and the dorms darkened early. He turned his desk lamp off and flopped onto his unmade bed. Only Teror's lamp remained on in the room, a single beacon failing to dissolve trespassing dark. "Theories are progressing here, but we have some questions."

Teror stared at him, reaching inside himself for some form of response that didn't come. It was automatic, this reaching. And it always neglected to reward him. The expectations of the self never met even Teror's lowest standards. If he'd cared, he might've become a maudlin boy, even depressed. He might even have become a serial killer. He met Harry's blue eyes. "What questions?"

"Have you ever tried to generate an emotion within yourself?"

"How do I try to feel something I do not understand?"

"How 'bout acting? Have you ever pretended you feel something then got wrapped up in the part?"

Teror shook his head.

"What about your studies? Your math courses. How do they make you feel?"

"Curiosity is all I have," Teror replied.

"Well, it's a place to start." Harry pursed his lips. "Curiosity *is* a feeling."

"But I don't know if I want to start," Teror said.

"You're missing out."

"I don't know that. You don't really know me. I can't miss something I never had."

"But don't you see the people around you? Don't you wonder? Isn't your curiosity driving you mad to learn, to know about love, hate, envy, anger…passion? Teror, you're a blank slate. You're only just beginning. It's wonderful. Don't you believe me? Don't you trust me?"

Harry had never lied to Teror. There was no reason not to believe in him, not to trust. The fact that it mattered to Harry meant that maybe it should matter to Teror. He reached. His response was still nothing.

"Well, we'll work on it," Harry said softly, perhaps disappointed, perhaps simply distant as he communed with the minds of his brothers.

"Shepherds wear robes 'cause sheep can hear a zipper a mile away. That's the joke. It's funny. Laugh!"

Teror sat cross-legged at the foot of his bed. Harry's blue eyes seemed to flicker in his face, mouth turned up, cheeks full, chuckles constricting his throat. Teror opened his mouth. "Ha-ha," he said stiffly, working hard on making his throat clench authentically.

"No. You're too self-conscious. Just let it go."

Teror tried again. "Eh-ha, eh-ha."

Harry sighed. "Better."

"Emotions seem to take a lot of time." Teror leaned, elbows on knees, chin in his hands.

"Well, yeah."

"They seem like a lot of excess mental clutter. Maybe I'm better the way I am."

"I don't believe that," Harry said.

"Well, then—" Teror hesitated. Finally, he said, "All right. I'll believe you."

30

"Keep it up. Use that belief and your curiosity. Use them to help you."

It wasn't working. Harry had shown him the funniest and saddest movies, tried to scare him on Halloween by staging a fake hanging in the dorm bathrooms, convinced a girl to seduce him—an evening that ended in utter disaster when Teror kept saying to her, "I don't care, whatever you want to do," and she stalked off muttering to herself about men being an alien species.

"My brothers and I have decided, after some thought and observation, that experience isn't enough to break through to you," Harry announced one afternoon.

Teror was in the middle of a physics problem, but didn't find the interruption of much consequence. He never lost his place where numbers and formulas were concerned. If Harry wanted to talk to him more about emotions, he could listen patiently for years if it took that long.

"My brothers and I have been discussing this bond we have," Harry continued. "You know, how we communicate over distance. We don't share only thoughts, but feelings, too. We've been questioning whether or not we could bring others into our group. You know, connect with them…touch minds."

"Like the old *Star Trek*. The mind-meld," Teror said helpfully.

Harry laughed, then instantly sobered. He stared at Teror for exactly ten seconds, as if Teror had changed somehow, become a different boy. "Yeah. Exactly like that."

"It's a painful experience, according to Spock," Teror informed. "But then you don't seem to be in pain with your brothers, and pain has no affect on me, so—"

"We were thinking of running a test."

"Okay."

"All fourteen of us are in agreement. We agreed that at six o'clock tonight we'd all concentrate on reaching out to you mentally, that we'd try to fill you with ourselves and see what happens."

Harry held his gaze for longer than seemed normal, then abruptly turned away. Teror's shoulders lifted in a shrug.

It was five minutes to six. "What should I do?" Teror asked.

"Maybe you should lie down."

"Will you have to touch me?" Teror went to his bed and reclined, head cushioned against a foam pillow.

Harry frowned. He stood at the foot of the bed, a presence that seemed to overflow the room and almost stifle Teror. For a moment, Teror couldn't breathe, then he felt his lungs inflate. "I don't think so," Harry answered.

"Good. I've had bad luck with touching. The other person always seems to get upset."

"You mean that night with Syndy."

"And other times."

Though Teror hadn't told Harry about any other times, Harry nodded as if he knew.

When six o'clock chimed across the campus from a nearby bell tower, Teror automatically closed his eyes. He didn't know why he did it. Perhaps for better concentration, perhaps to present to the fourteen Aaron clones as blank a surface as they might ever meet.

At first he felt a tickle, like a little breath, an errant breeze filtering through his brain. There were voices, but he couldn't make out any words. Some laughter. A sound like a man calling to another person across an abyss. A great rush of light, like a thousand fireflies swarming. The buzz and clatter of machinery in a closed room. The breach of light returned again and again, twisting through him in awe. There was no pain. No sensation of a deeper communication with whatever flashed through him. Nothing.

The atmosphere quieted. He heard a sound outside his mind, beyond the edge of the dark, and opened his eyes.

Harry sat on the edge of his bed, dark head bent, hair twisting over hands that pressed his face. The sound came again, strangled breath, drawn air through damp sinuses.

"Are you crying?" Teror asked, sitting up gracefully, drawing his legs under him and placing his hands neatly on his thighs.

Harry pushed back his thick hair. His blue eyes were red-rimmed. "We took you into us and there was nothing."

"Oh."

"Well, not nothing," Harry went on, voice thick in his throat. "Memories. A chaos of numbers which seems to be your chief focus. At least you have that. And curiosity. But nothing else."

"You are surprised?" Teror asked.

"I thought there would be something of you that could reach forward, reach out to us. But there was nothing. Just your experiences as if set aside, belonging to someone else." Dark eyebrows narrowed. "You really let a girl almost drown? And you let a guy rape you?"

"Yes, those things happened," Teror said.

"How terrible." He was silent a moment, his mouth set, cheeks puffed with studious attention. "Now more than ever we're determined to help. It's for your own protection. And others. But first, you. You have no self-preservation. You'd let someone shoot you down without a fight. That's not right."

"But you said there's nothing there to see. The experiment failed."

"I'm not giving up yet. We'll just have to put something there."

"But—"

"But nothing. There's a soul in you. Everyone has one. I can see it in you sometimes. I know I'm not hallucinating."

33

"When? When have you seen this thing?" Teror asked. Curiosity came over him with shocking strength. Was this what it was like to feel? Could desperation be like this? As quickly, the thought was gone. It didn't matter. Nothing ever did.

"Right now. Your curiosity is you. Is your soul. I just have to figure it out."

Teror moved to his desk, waved on his computer and opened a file of homework. But a remainder of curiosity made him turn, made him study the young man on the bed. There were fourteen of him. None of those Aarons had ever known the beauty of blankness, of being on the edge, of what existence alone was like. Now they had gotten a taste. "Were you really crying for me?" Teror asked.

"Of course," Harry said, slipping into his vacant, pondering pose.

Teror had never seen Harry so upset. The charmer of the dorms had darkened over the winter months. He seemed obsessed with working on Teror's problem. Harry's grades dropped, and Teror could only watch his roommate grow more and more restless, and the distant look came into the blue eyes often now as he seemed to draw into himself and his brothers in lieu of parties, classes, even meals.

For weeks, they did not try the mind-meld again, and Harry never spoke of it. But Teror suspected that was what was on Harry's mind, and what all his brothers thought about and discussed.

Early winter froze the landscape, made everything white and bleak, even the sky which seemed like a frosted window that wouldn't open, that would never know heat again.

Neither Teror nor Harry left for the holidays. Harry had been one of the fourteen who had never been adopted, and his foster homes had branded no familial imprint on him.

He didn't need to see his brothers; he was with them all the time. And so both stayed in the dorm while the scent of pine garlands and holly decorations on the stairs assailed them, making Teror feel colder, Harry neglected.

On Christmas day, Harry handed a wrapped present to Teror. "I know you can't understand why I wanted to give you something, but take it anyway. Because I want you to."

Teror unwrapped the box. Inside was an old abacus, the beads slick with wear but still painted a strong, glowing black. "This is inefficient," Teror said.

"Yes, I know." Harry crossed his arms. "That's the point. So many things are. It's okay, too."

"It didn't occur to me to get anything for you. The holiday means nothing to me. And I don't know what I'd get for anyone if I did think of it."

"You've already given me something. You make me think. And think." A small smile touched the full lips. "Despite it all, I like you, Teror."

"Okay," Teror said. He felt himself reach again into a place deep inside himself for another stronger response his body and even his intellect seemed instinctively to demand, but there was nothing.

The part of him that reached seemed to wither with a kind of regret. But he could not know if it was real regret or the simple thought of it. Then Teror wondered if he'd been looking in the wrong place. The reaching part strengthened and moved up, parting through the nothingness like a rod of invisible energy, churned through organs, blood, flesh, dusted the surface of Teror's skin with a static charge that flicked outward. If there had been sparks, they would have been green, licking like split demon tongues at his hands, his face, then flaring, elfin lightning spears aimed at Harry.

"Teror?" Harry questioned.

Teror's hand came up, fingers extended. "Just a touch?"

"What?" But as Harry's forehead wrinkled, his own hand came up, mirror to Teror's. Their fingertips touched.

More than light flitted through Teror's mind this time, more than tickles on the brain. Fire roared. Burned. Silk fire both hurting and comforting. And so many aches and pressures he thought he would die. In a single moment images ruptured almost too quick to capture: a kiss that blossomed on the body and spun the mind, a fear that froze every cell, pain that ate the victim alive, joy that felt like flying and warmth, love that smelled of sweet air, the distracting pang of envy, despair like a closet door locked against the heart.

"Oh," said Teror, and his knees buckled.

Harry caught him as he fell. The abacus hit the floor and broke, spreading black beads everywhere.

"You did it," Harry was saying. "You did. You were experiencing it. What I am. What all humans are!"

Teror lay on his bed. His legs and arms felt weak, chilled.

"You did. You felt it," Harry repeated. "Tell me. Tell me you did."

"I did."

"Yes!" Harry clapped his hands together.

Teror looked up at him. "That was what you wanted for me? To feel like that is good?"

Harry froze, frowned. "You didn't think so?"

"It was too much. I couldn't think anymore."

"It's not always like that. You just got it all in one strong dose. We have to learn to leach it to you a little at a time, that's all."

"I don't know. It wasn't pleasant."

"Not any of it?"

"I don't know."

"That's just it. You don't know. It's all so new. But you're still curious, aren't you?"

Teror had never felt more tired. He turned away from Harry, onto his side. "I have to sleep," he said quietly.

He dreamed the scene again. Only this time it was different. When his fingers touched Harry's, Harry became like him, empty. No more smiles. No more sparkles in the blue eyes, or dark, distant poses. Next, the thirteen brothers were affected. All went out into the world, and whatever they touched grew calm, still. Light wavered but did not dance. There was no more pain, no more war. Love died. Happiness was not a concern because all human life had comfort and security. With that, everything was all right. Harry and Teror and the rest of the world could live together in flat-lined peace.

When Teror woke from his nap, Harry was there, staring at him. "My brothers and I are developing more theories," he said, grinning. He looked so alive, blended with the world in a way Teror never noticed before. Christmas was waning, but the glitter of Harry had been reborn.

"Oh."

"We think you can train yourself to learn to take only what you need, what you want from others. From us."

"I don't think it's such a good idea." He swung his legs over the side of the bed and stood.

"You believe in me, don't you?"

Teror always had. For some reason unknown to him, some motive neither curiosity nor intellect could define, he held a belief, a stray alien interest in Harry's philosophies, Harry's emotional phenomena. "Yes."

The siphoning began with all the brothers concentrating at once on a single thread of emotion. The emotion: Happiness. They each focused on what they liked to do: bowling, driving fast, painting, running laps, eating ice cream, winning a contest, screaming into wind, making love.

Teror reached up, out, his hand encountering Harry's with a shock that ran through his whole body and continued to fill him with that crazy surging current they called joy.

The only problem occurred when Teror and Harry stopped touching. When the current ceased, so did all emotion. Teror could retain none of it.

"Maybe it'll just take some time," Harry said.

"Maybe." Teror had the memory of emotion, but could conjure no joy of his own.

"Your mind just needs to get used to feeling, to absorbing feeling."

Teror believed in him.

They kept trying. By spring they were exhausted and their grades were falling. There were sun and flowers, little storms, a whole shining world waiting to be won. But the experiments took nearly all their free time.

Teror found himself craving the emotions Harry gave. Was "craving" a feeling? He thought not. The brothers, being distant and having full lives themselves, only rarely participated now, having lost some of their interest, but Harry and Teror discovered they didn't need them. Harry could fill Teror himself, his emotional realm unlimited.

"I want to feel that again," Teror said.

"At least you can feel need," Harry muttered tiredly.

"It is good. I believe in you. Just give me more."

They'd been connected for an hour. Harry had homework. Teror hadn't slept much the night before. But Harry had devoted himself to this project. To Teror. "All right. Come here."

Harry learned what Teror's favorites were. Excitement: they would watch movies together and share the suspense, the thrill. Obsession: Harry would share whatever new things stayed on his mind, a baseball game, a good book, pining after a girl. Sensual desire: This one made Harry uncomfortable at first. Lying in bed one night when he'd thought Teror was asleep, he began to masturbate. "Please," Teror said into the darkness. The next day the moved the beds side by side, leaving space between them for privacy. Then at night, Harry would reach his hand out between the space. Teror would grasp it, and know pleasure.

The homework rarely got done.

It only occurred to Harry after spring was almost over that Teror had become addicted to his emotions. The addiction was irrational, since Teror still experienced no feelings of his own, but it was there. Teror had become filled, but with need only, and no way on his own to quench that emotional rift within. Since Harry needed to be needed, he didn't mind Teror's demands.

When the school year ended, they took an apartment together and got part time jobs. Their relationship precluded outside attachments.

"Sometimes I resent you," Harry told Teror one day.

"I know."

"But then I realize I need your need and it's all I want."

"I know."

Harry smiled. When he touched Teror's hand, Teror smiled back.

One day, Harry came home from work at the wrong time. His face looked wan. His eyes held darknesses that Teror had known before and never liked.

Teror followed him into their bedroom. "This is bad. I can tell. What happened?" He thought he was learning some empathy, though only the kind where the empathizer gets the reward. Or perhaps it was just the old curiosity.

"One of my brothers was killed in a plane crash."

Teror did not know what to say.

"A part of myself has died." Harry sat on the bed, fingers clutching at the bedspread.

"You're still alive. You'll recover."

Harry only turned away, lying down on the worn sheets. "Just leave me alone."

Teror left. He made dinner. When he came back into their bedroom, Harry was sobbing. "We all felt it," he explained. He wasn't hungry, so Teror ate alone.

That night, there was no connecting for the first time since Christmas.

Harry did not improve the next day. His brothers and he were all depressed, all feeding off each other until the misery could not be controlled. It drowned them. Teror touched him once, reaching out, then withdrew immediately as though burned. Harry's pain was not something he wanted. Ever.

If Harry didn't get over this soon, he would have to find a replacement. He coldly informed Harry of this. But things did not change.

After two weeks of chronic depression, Harry came to Teror, gaunt, hair dirty, sweat pants falling low on his hips. "Don't go looking for a replacement yet. My brothers and I have a theory," he said.

"Another one?" Teror watched the blue eyes, trying to read what was there, wishing in his strange addiction he could just fall into them again. And again.

"You can help us."

"How?"

Harry explained.

It was hard not to reach out, not to take. Teror had grown used to it. Taking love, thieving joy, lifting thrills from Harry's mind and transferring them to his own. Giving to

Harry was a different matter altogether. He'd done it once, shared his blank self, but that had been a long time ago, and seemed to fail.

But now, the reaching out part of him, the part that had learned selfish want and need, went inward to the deep source of nothingness he ascribed as his true identity, to the so-called soul he carried that had no weight, no acknowledgment, no existence save that it had formed him, had made him into such a being who could not feel unless he sucked stimulation from others. He went into his vampire self and waited.

The lights that represented the essences of the clone brothers appeared to him in his mind. From his empty prison, he took them in. He held them in his arms, thirteen fireflies passing through the nothingness around him, then landing upon his soul, feeding.

Give, give, they seemed to say. *Give us calm. We're tired. We need to rest from the horror of death, of all emotion.*

It was easy. He held Harry and the brothers in his hollow embrace, and poured his indifference upon them. It wouldn't be permanent, but it was a beginning. Later, maybe they could learn to enfold that void within their own hearts. If not, they'd most certainly become addicted to it—addiction was in their Aaron genes. Then they'd do anything—laugh for him, cry for him, love, hate—to feel again what Teror could give.

Bitters

He could not get enough of love.

In San Diego, lovers filled the malls, the boardwalks, and the gas lamp district of downtown where horse-drawn carriages ambled by Horton Plaza and Seaport Village taking tourists to the waterfront. Malachi bought a ride on one of them, and the driver, Beth, with her chestnut horse, Tiffini, drove him past docked Navel ships, harbor cruise boats and seafood restaurants, all the while chatting and laughing on her walkie-talkie to other buggy drivers.

Malachi didn't mind the chatter. In fact, he was glad she didn't try to draw him into fake amenities. Falseness always hit him with a bitter coating in the back of his throat. He could not abide it, and all the lies; so many terrible lies like puncture wounds to the heart filled the world where humans lived. He preferred instead to succumb to the lull of the horse's hooves on the hot black pavement, to the salty air that caught and curled his long hair, to the beating sunlight as it boiled through him, making his skin feel clean and malleable and alive.

But the hunger was there, too. Pleasant as this was, total relaxation was difficult because he was alone, because no loving couple waited for him in his fancy hotel suite, because true to the cliché: Love could not be forced, bargained for, or bought.

As the buggy carried him forward, Malachi's gaze caught on a young couple emerging from a card shop. In a flash, he saw their history. A full moon night where they'd consummated their love on the beach. Gestures of mingling. Shared midnight phone conversations. Lunches at a middle school. They'd been childhood sweethearts. Best friends, too. Full, they were. Blooming. Begging to be picked.

He could feel their passion even at this distance. It went beyond their simple body language, fingers woven together as the male, wavering in his tremendous height, leaned toward the female where her shoulder brushed his bicep. The stirring brought him forward, his hand coming to lie gently on Beth's back.

"Stop here," Malachi said.

"What?" The girl turned in her seat as the horse stopped, munching quietly on its bit.

"Wait, please," he said. "I'll be right back."

He jumped from the back seat and moved forward, the people surging, everywhere cotton candy and popcorn and blistering light and the sea. And then there was their love. The closer he got to them, the quicker he moved. They were gravity to him. They were confection. He came up behind them where they stood in each other's heat, gazing into a window of goodies they really didn't see. Their thoughts were on each other, erotic images that lightly sunned Malachi even as their delight, while he absorbed, pumped through him like a drug.

He let it feed him. His hand reached out, instinct and fervor, and he touched the back of the man's shoulder with the flat of his palm. He felt the faint shock of his touch ripple along the skin and through his hand. The man turned into the hand, facing him, muscles tensing, eyebrows verging together.

Quickly, Malachi said, "Mark?" He smiled, lowering his gaze until his lashes shadowed his eyes. "Oh, excuse me. I thought you were someone I knew."

"Of course." The frown turned from fear to puzzlement, and finally, as their eyes met, to forgiveness.

Instant gratification. Oranges and honey tanged the air. Alabaster daylight along with this man and woman—she now turning away from the window to see who her husband was talking to—were the perfect complimentary courses in his temporary snack.

The man's eyes took him in with instant acceptance. The woman was drawn to him as well, pulse gripping veins in a flutter of curiosity and appreciation. They had already been aroused by each other. He merely enhanced that sensation, feeling it through his palm as he let it drop, energy throbbing up his arm to his throat, his chest, his heart.

Malachi bowed his head. "My apologies for the error."

"No problem," the man said. The woman's smile followed him all the way back to the carriage.

This was what Malachi fed on. This, and sunlight. Neither were traditionally a vampire's friend. But Malachi was rarely traditional.

He knew no one else who was like him. No creature who tasted and drank as he did of longing and allegiance, passion and sensuality. Committed couples, those who were married, or who shared some long term history together, gave off the most delectable of flavors. Gay and straight couples were quite equal in their fervor, and his palette did not discriminate among them. It was the commitment he craved, the sharing between them, the merging. Love was a fascination all its own, attached by a thread sometimes, other times fastened like a vise onto couples who visited its gold and blue world, who lapped at its rivers, who sucked the elixir air. To be a seeker of that world, and yet never able to visit there himself, was Malachi's torment. Sometimes he would be accepted by a couple for their lifetime, until they died; other times he would stay only a night, savoring them on his lips and skin the way he savored the sun.

He never aged. He never died. He could remember a vague childhood in ancient Egypt, but not the dates. How old was he? Three millennia? Four? He'd stopped counting. Or caring. He told everyone he was thirty-one. Year in and year out, that number never changed. *He* never changed, his bronze hair, his black deep-set eyes, his nearly hairless skin that soaked up the sunlight as if light were all that made up his muscles and sinew and bones.

Beyond his childhood, there was a time when he hadn't always been like this. Vampire, yes. Living in light, no. To remember that harsher era sickened him, the distinct edge of power and horror that came to him when he had once drifted and lapped at another's pain, at death, at greed. How many dark streets had he tainted with his shadow side, yearning to drink a lost boy's hunger, a widow's grief, a young man's suicidal dive off a haunted bridge? How disgusted he had been with himself even as he took pleasure from the murder of a babe. It was an addiction to top himself night after night, to not only taste, but rule the inky recesses of ultimate thrills and lusts, greed and power.

There was still evil within him. Still parts of himself that curdled and whined for wilder, animal passions. A smile tickled his lips, but he was under perfect control. He was strong. He glanced out to the rich azure Pacific to cleanse his mind. The young couple's creamy taste still lingered and he did not want to spoil it.

In the day's glow the ocean looked like a flood of rippling blue sparks. With each lick of the shore, it seemed to chant: *Something lost, something gained.* He knew only too well the meaning of that litany.

The horse's hooves clopped along the blacktop, and a wind ruffled her mane. Her fancy bridle, gold and silver with studded fake gemstones, kept flashing in Malachi's eyes. The tide lapped at the hulls on boats at the docks, making a sucking sound. Children with ice cream cones ran along the boardwalk, shouting. White gulls called out with yelping voices to the tide and the pale sky beyond.

Lost in this paradise, this tourist-lover's world, Malachi's hunger slept, temporarily sated. He let his eyes shift from scene to scene.

Strange faces, strange conversations. Suddenly, one of the faces stood out of the throng, too familiar, too known.

Stunned, Malachi sat bolt upright in his seat. It couldn't be. Nemesis. Tempter. Perry!

The boy wore tight spandex bicycle shorts and a black tank top. His brown hair was pushed back into a loose ponytail to reveal a perfect hairline. He walked easily in the crowd, though he was no native, and no tourist to be sure. No. Malachi had known Perry as a neighbor since the kid was six years old. The orphan waif had wandered into the village of Tania where Malachi had lived for centuries, and been taken in by a farmer family down the road. The boy had survived God-knew-what to mature into the cagey, very natural predator he was. This kid had learned never to take no for an answer, unless "no" was his idea.

Malachi drew in a sharp breath, teeth clenching until they ached. The first time he'd ever encountered this neighbor boy face to face, Perry had been about ten. He'd come down the stairs in his modest estate to find an angelic-faced child going through the drawers of an end table he sometimes used as a desk. He'd recognized him as the farmer's adopted son and, outraged, had come up behind him, soft as air, picking him up by the collar of his shirt. The boy had yelped and squirmed, literally turning in his clothes to face his adversary.

"What are you doing in my house?" Malachi demanded.

The reply from the pouting mouth was not what he'd expected. Instead of fear, the kid retorted, "Waiting to see how long it would take you to catch me."

He'd been overwhelmed by the crudity, then, and the child's desperate yearnings that already at age ten were dark and selfish and tinged with a sinister lust. The kid was everything Malachi avoided, dangled like some obscene lure to shatter his current regimen.

That had been ten years ago.

Now Malachi leaned over Beth with a hundred dollar bill in his hand, and said, "Stop here. I have to get off here."

Beth, frowning, pulled back on Tiffini's reins. "What?" Her curls framed a full, pink face. Another time, he might have found it intriguing.

"Keep the change," Malachi called over his shoulder. His sandaled feet hit the pavement with a slap. A red Volkswagen slowed as it passed, honking, drawing attention to him.

At that moment, Perry's eyes met his and he stopped on the sidewalk, crowds moving around him in a never receding current. The boy grinned, white teeth like separate entitles flashing. Malachi grimaced. To think this "child" had followed him all the way from that backwoods village to this city.

Perry had been one of the reasons Malachi decided to leave the older country for awhile. Young Perry had been far too curious at first. Then, later, too demanding in his voracious perseverance to draw Malachi to him. Now, it irritated him to think this slippery boy could so easily track him. And where, by the gods, had he gotten the money? Surely not from his peasant farmer of a father.

Malachi turned away from the boy and crossed the street, heading back toward Seaport Village and, hopefully, a little anonymity.

"Malachi! Stop! Dammit!" came the expected call. His English was good for a scant twenty year-old wiseacre who, a year ago, had spoken only Austrian. The accent was even kind of cute, a regular Van Damme pitch.

Malachi winced even as a flutter of hunger moved within him. Endearing on the surface, Perry would no doubt take up where he'd left of in Tania, bulldozing his way through Malachi's life. Too often, he felt responsible for him. Perry was always making the most wicked of choices, but that wasn't Malachi's fault. He had to keep telling himself that.

But still, something inside him made him stop, allow the kid to catch him, do his dance in his tight little shorts and grin and bow and thrust out his chin. "Choose me," was what the act translated to. The boy could be so shockingly arrogant!

He turned just in time to see Perry dodge a bicycler. A sudden gust of wind pushed through the rigging on the *Star of India* docked behind him, and the ropes and pulleys of the old iron sail boat rattled like an omen.

Perry jogged across the wide street, stopping a few feet away from Malachi, tilting his head. "Exquisite," he said, his accent almost charming. Then he switched to Austrian. "I couldn't stand it a minute more at home. Farming!" He almost spit. "So I sold some of the jewelry you left behind in your safe. You don't mind, do you?" He shrugged, still smiling, and held up his right hand. "Oh, all except for this." On his middle finger was a fire opal set in smooth, highly polished gold. "I liked it too much. It reminds me of you. Burning but contained."

Malachi couldn't even breathe for a moment. No one knew about his safe. Not even the last couple who'd lived with him, and who'd both died so early and so quickly in a rock slide in Tania's Rainbird Hills. Perry had been nineteen then, and yes, a bitter snoop who, after years of preparing himself to be one of Malachi's next companions, had nearly devoured himself in his own anger when he had not been chosen.

He remembered that day as if it had just passed. It was an honor to be chosen by Tania's resident legend, the rich prince who presided over nothing in their tiny little square of world. In the line-up of hopefuls, their faces expectant and pampered, had slouched irascible Perry, sullen, beautiful but still, even after Malachi made it clear what was required, darkly irreverent, exuding only selfish desires, never real love.

When Perry had made it known to Malachi that he was grooming himself to participate in the next village line-up, Malachi had actually tried to help him succeed.

"I want a pair," he told him.

"But I could be all you need," countered the boy. "Then you could make me like you, and we could be companions forever."

"No. I cannot."

"No?" Insolent, never shy. "You made those rules. Change them."

Malachi could feel the encompassing contamination of rage at the memory. "Find a girl, or a boy—" he'd begun.

"But they all hate me." And with those words, Perry had brushed off any concern for what Malachi needed or wanted. "It's better that way anyway. I don't like any of them, either. Only you. Because I want to be like you."

"You'll fail," Malachi had told him.

"Not if you see that I don't." Then he'd put on the charm again, nineteen and full of energy and lust and those angelic cheeks, full mouth, skin like melting honey. He had felt the hunger come on, then, sharp and tormenting.

"Come on," Perry had said. "You know you like me just the way I am. And you *can* choose me."

Malachi had experienced a momentary weakness that made him actually consider it for a moment. The baby-orphan had turned into a young man that deviled him, went for every vulnerability he had, and despite himself, Malachi was intrigued, a compassion welling, and a kind of love that kept company with danger. But he was done with that part of his life. Darkness held nothing for him anymore. He had changed. He knew if he chose Perry, the kid would ruin him, because Perry had no ability to give in the manner Malachi now craved. The brat had set himself up to fail.

Now he looked at the hand Perry held up to his face, the opal burning the air like a miniature nova, and for the first time Malachi felt genuine anger at this kid for his immaturity, for his lack of a conscience.

Malachi's hand shot out and gripped Perry's fingers hard, twisting the ring off the middle finger without regard to the pain it might cause. "You sold my belongings? I *do* mind!"

The touch was anathema to his will. Clinging hatreds and resentments and furies threatened to pull him over to Perry's world. Enticing memory of long-past darker times. He pushed the kid's hand away then, clutching the ring in his fist. The anger he felt, the loathing at Perry's actions, emptied him of all resonance of what made him the kind of man he was now. He felt bereft, hollow, torn. Invaded. A part of him withered. And this was exactly what Perry wanted.

Perry made a fist with his injured hand, but the pain did not appear to distract him. "You have someone else, then?" he asked in Austrian. His eyes were a bright, pale gray. "Not someone better than me. That could never be." There was a pause, a little frown. "Could it?"

Taken aback by those last words, Malachi did not know how to respond.

After the too-long silence, Perry's frown reversed to a smile. "You don't answer. That's good. That means you haven't found anyone else." The smile lifted the pink lips. "I have it all figured out, you know. Don't you understand anything? Why I followed you here? Why I had to sell your stuff to get the money? I'm sorry about that, but you can't deny me my life, Mal."

Malachi flinched. He hated that nickname.

"I never intended to be one of your mindless pawns," Perry continued. "I won't let you turn your back on me. I don't want to die, and you have that secret. I'm more like you than you are, and that scares you. You recognize it. You always have. You can't deny me life!"

"I have no knowledge of that," Malachi insisted. He'd been asked this before, through the millennia. By the lovers who kept him filled. By the rare friend. But the answer was always the same. He'd been born this way, as far as he knew. He was who he was, which could not be helped.

'You just don't want to see what you are. And you don't want to look because I threaten to show it to you." Perry put a hand on his hip. His black shorts shone like a blind mirror. "You're the carnivore that pretends to be a vegetarian. You have more power than you're admitting, or allowing."

"No! You don't know anything of what you're saying."

"Don't I?"

"Now who's making up rules?" Malachi asked. "You have your ideas, and that's all they are."

He laughed. "But they make you furious."

"Because you don't know anything! You're making it all up."

"I'm looking at you, aren't I? You're not a figment of my imagination. You're here. Alive. Ageless. Is it a crime for me to want that, too?"

"But I can't provide it! Even if I could love you—" He stopped abruptly. A few passersby glanced up at him, then were swept away by their personal agendas.

Perry drew closer to him, scent of salt and sweat, of spicy shampoo and a cool mouth. "Then" he said slowly, "I'll die. And you don't want that." An irresistible potency flamed in Perry.

Malachi forced himself to ignore it. "As all humans do." But there was a longing in his voice. And every time he pulled away from him like this, it was as if a little more of Perry lodged in him, making him angry, frustrated, tense. And every time, a little more of his resistance was chipped down, revealing what he'd taken hundreds of years to obscure. It wasn't love between them, but it was a connection of souls just as powerful.

As if reading his thoughts, Perry said slowly, "You realize you don't love me only because you're just as incapable of it as I am. We're so alike, only you deny your nature."

"I am not a beast! I choose."

"Yeah. Sure."

Not wanting to hear any more, he turned and started up the sidewalk. He felt the presence even as he expected it.

Perry shadowing him. Perry keeping up the pace, never letting him go.

"Prince Malachi," he said. This time the voice was less arrogant, more desperate. But only, he knew, because Perry stood to lose. "I'll pay you back. I'm sorry I pawned your things. But I had to see you. My life is nothing but a blink of your eye. I've never accepted that. And I never will!"

"I don't have your answers. And I don't care about the money. Here." As he walked, he thrust out the opal ring "Take this and use it to get home." He would not meet the kid's eyes. *Go away*, he thought. *Just go away.*

But his demands were a little like telling the sun to turn off. The force. The pull. How he hated Perry for doing this to him.

Perry did not immediately reach for the ring. "I'm not going home. I'm going to Los Angeles. I'm going to be an actor. And I will pay you back."

Malachi spun, stopping them both. They stood in front of a little seafood restaurant that stank of dead fish. A panhandler sat at the curb, head down, a paper McDonald's cup thrust up. "So then I guess you don't need the ring?" He glanced from the beggar to Perry, then back at the beggar.

Perry lowered his eyes, and Malachi felt safe for the moment to look at him. He really was a sight. Chiseled jaw line. Light brown hair that made itself gold and red in the light. Arms and legs tight as steel from all the farm work he'd grown up doing.

When Perry didn't answer him, he said, "Fine." And reached over and dropped the opal ring into the panhandler's cup. The man barely looked up, as if he hadn't realized yet what fortune had been placed in his hand.

Perry's eyes widened. Perfect teeth caught at a pink lower lip.

"But--?"

"You act the part, but you are not the part," Malachi said to him, then he turned and strode south, the darkness in him almost a pain now. He needed love. And he needed it fast.

He did not look behind him as he turned the corner and headed, at a clipped pace, toward his hotel.

He would have preferred a hearth fire to assuage the pain night brought, but the suite was not equipped with a fireplace. Instead, Malachi turned up the heat and kept all the lights on. He lit candles which, for his own pleasure, fed him the light he needed so much after the sun left for the day. He kept the plush pink curtains closed on the dark. He swathed his body in white. White linen button-up shirt, white brushed-silk trousers. The splash of a ruby ring on his right hand, and a ruby broach at his collar, were the only stains that interrupted the flow of paleness. His bronze hair, thick at the nape, had been pulled back into a braid; he'd tied it off with near-invisible white thread.

He couldn't go out like this, he knew. He looked ridiculous, like someone from a play about God and his assistants, someone who hadn't yet removed his performer persona.

So he stayed in, though after Perry, his hunger had increased. Lounging on a hard, uncomfortable couch, he wondered how long he could go without the more permanent aura of those who could feed him what he wanted. A meeting in a street, a brushing of his body against lovers on the sidewalk could only sustain him for a few moments. He couldn't keep that essence. There were simply too many negative draws that polluted it. He'd never gone for more than a year in the past without some more permanent arrangement of love. Without partners, he'd been far from himself from lack of sustenance, like a man suffering grief, blanched by loss of will. This made him all too susceptible to past horrors.

After the sudden deaths of his last couple, Marie and Jacques, only months ago, he'd been stricken with a pain that left him only when the sun was full on him, radiating fire-heat. Their sudden accident had half-destroyed him. He'd only known them a short while, but their love had been young and hot and addictive. And they were not inhibited—even eighteen –year-old Jacques had the manner of a secure, mid-thirties gentleman—nor were they intimidated by Malachi's presence in the velvet bed he'd had custom made for them.

Gods, those bright days in slippery silk, those moments of never-ending passion that fed him in a rush of drowning euphoria.

Marie and Jacques, like so many of his young mates, thought at first he had intended a three-way sexual union. But Malachi did not need to be touched.

Marie and Jacques would crawl into the crooks of his arms, try to draw him in, but always, after a few minutes of giving them the affection and reassurance humans seem to need, Malachi pushed them away and encouraged their separate union.

In that heat, he basked, the memory of them so close, and so far.

"Come here to me, Jacques," he heard Marie say. The room echoed with her primrose scent.

Malachi's dream-ghost's haunted the air.

And as Jacques obeyed, breathing, "Yes," they both called out his name, one voice low and rumbling, the other whispery with awe. "Malachi," they said, bodies meeting. "Malachi."

He felt himself open up like a flower to the sun, his body rippling with their desires. He feasted on remembered energy, feeling it course through him and renew his cells, his mind, his soul. The psychic flow had been so strong, he never had to watch them to reach his peak of pleasure, but most of his couples grew to desire his audience, and were offended if he closed his eyes.

The phantoms Jacques and Marie drew him in by making love over his body. How many times had they done this, how many times had they collapsed on top of him, giggling or moaning, or silent in the face of such enormous rapture. The wonder, then. He could not contain it.

Tears slipped from his eyes; his body rippled, erect and engorged, for what seemed like hours of dreamy ecstasy.

"Malachi," Marie whispered. "Malachi," Jacques echoed.

At times such as these, he could barely stand to be touched. His own orgasms were mere stirrings in comparison to what he felt when his lovers climaxed. He never fed on himself; that was a lost course. But when they began to moan and touch, lick and tease, he drank and felt himself as vibrant a part of the immortal universe as a star, or a galaxy of stars.

On quieter days, he would feel like a glutton on a shared glance, a smile, a look.

After he'd lost Marie and Jacques, the village of Tania seemed to close in on him too tight, to hold him in a kind of stasis he felt compelled to fight. He decided to leave his home for the first time in over 200 years, venture into the world. He was not a traveler. The roots in Tania were deep.

So far, San Diego had given up none of its souls to him.

Now rain tapped lightly at the closed window of the room. Dampness and darkness. Malachi shivered, all the ghosts vanished for now, and drew his white form closer to the three candles on the low table before him. The air blazed with light. The flames of the candles were shaped like tiny white upside-down hearts. He raised his hands over them and let them singe the sensitive skin of his palms. Light was a poor substitute for love, but it was good. It was a drink that could satiate him. For a little while.

Heat wavered through the room. The scent of melting wax became his breath, became his center. He closed his eyes, put up his white stockinged feet and tried to relax, to force the pain of negative dregs to recede.

Too often these days the negative energy tried to fill his chest. The refuse of falseness, of endings and lies, sent arrows of agony into his lungs. The taste of gloom would chafe at the back of his throat, taunting. Light made the foulness weaken.

Love, if he could have found any tonight, would have obliterated it.

Perry had no idea what he was asking of him. Selfish boy. Irritant. Imp.

Malachi breathed in slowly, then out. Eventually, he could fall asleep this way, and be comforted by the dawn. If, that was, the storm let up.

He kept his eyes closed and tried again to remember better times. But Perry's face kept stippling itself on the insides of his eyelids. Love. Was there any of that in him which he hadn't gleaned from other sources? Any that he could call his own?

A sharp rap at the door jarred him from his pose. He got up, straightening his clothing, and opened the door.

"Speak of the devil and he shall appear," Malachi said.

Perry, soaked through, ponytail sticking to his bare shoulder, stood at the threshold, shivering, a small sack cloth draped over his arm.

Malachi's stomach clenched on too much emptiness. Something of the orphan from fourteen years ago glanced briefly from under spiky, damp bangs.

"I can never run far enough. Creatures such as you will always find me," he added, and stood back and ushered the waif in. "Actor, indeed." He closed the door and crossed his arms.

Perry tried to puff out his chest in protest, but it was laughable in his drenched condition. "Just for tonight," he said in slow English. "I am going to L.A."

It didn't surprise Malachi that Perry had followed him back to his hotel. But it did surprise him to see the opal again on Perry's middle finger. The fire twitched against his knuckles. Perry, almost dry now, sat in a white hotel-provided robe surveying the overly lit room.

"How can you stand it? It's just not you. Not the real you. All this light! Ah, I need those...those what do you call them things? Eye-coverings." Perry squinted at the candelabra that decorated one brocaded table.

"Sunglasses," Malachi said, providing the English term. "Speak in Austrian if you prefer." He held his hands together tightly in his lap. It kept them from shaking.

"Whatever." He shaded his eyes with one hand and stared at Malachi.

Malachi looked away from Perry's intense gaze and drew his feet up under him on the couch. "You can sleep in my room for tonight. I'll sleep out here."

"I can sleep out here," Perry said. "If you put out these lights, that is. You know I prefer it dark."

"And I prefer it light."

Perry let out a puff of breath. "Yeah, I know."

Malachi rolled his eyes. Perry's answer for everything was: I know this; I know that; I know all. He should never have invited him in. He should have chased him away that first day he'd caught him stealing in his house. He should have thrashed the boy.

As if reading his thoughts, Perry said suddenly, "You know, when I was a kid the other boys were afraid of you. The first time I broke into your house, it was one of those dares boys make. I wasn't scared. They called you warlock even while the folks were calling you 'prince'. I didn't believe either one."

"I only did good for the village. All the children saw that."

"Yeah, food for the poorer families, toys for the kids. I know. All in exchange for two of us when you decided you wanted us. How much is a human life worth, hmm?"

"I do not take human life."

"So you say."

Malachi's heartbeat surged with his temper. How easily Perry could bring this out in him. How cruelly.

"I wonder what death would taste of," Perry continued. "You do drink of us, so you could know."

"I don't care or wonder what the taste would be like," he shot back. "Stop it. You know what you do to me. So just stop."

Perry's eyebrows lifted in pretend innocence.

"Why can't you ever say anything nice? I swear I oughta…" Malachi turned away, stared at the blue and white undulation of one candle.

"Oughta what? Wash my mouth out? Take me over your knee?" He laughed sharply, but only once. "Go ahead, Mr. Pure of Heart. You want to. You want to do far more than that, Mr. I Can't Get Enough of Love. What do you think love is?" He snickered.

"Whatever it is, it isn't in you. And I can't teach it to you."

"Then teach me what you do know. Your true nature. That's what I recognize. That's what I need."

"You're fantasizing," Malachi countered.

"Can I ask you a question, then?"

"No." He clenched his hands tighter together.

Ignoring the unwanted answer, Perry said, "Didn't you ever think that by keeping your secret all to yourself, you're condemning humanity just as if you'd murdered them with your own hands?"

"No." He pushed himself up as the denial reverberated through the room, paced to the curtained window where raindrops battered glass with a tin-drum sound. He could smell the rain, like torture throughout his whole body. Like all the things Perry was trying to awaken with his perverse little soul. The dark outside suckled at him with the mouths of a million tiny demons. Perry had brought some of those mouths into the hotel with him, back into Malachi's heart. Those devils that had instructed the boy to chase Malachi for ten

58

years, those devils that made Perry want to spread his malignant enticements.

There was silence behind him for a long time. But he could feel the natural lurking mind of Perry, the pale eyes glaring at the back of his head.

Finally, Perry spoke. Softly. The voice almost an echo of the outside wind. "I want you."

Malachi fell forward on the sill, legs almost giving way, and stifled a groan. Pain gutted him.

Then, from his side, he felt a touch, a hand under his elbow, another against his back. "You do have feelings," Perry said after a chuckle.

"Damn you!" He whirled, pushing Perry aside. "You want to ruin me. Why? Why can't you learn I don't want what you are? Why do you keep coming back?" He pushed past the hands, not seeing the boy anymore, or the bright flickers of light that made up the room.

"Because I can. Because I know your spirit, and how you try to hide it with all the frills and lace and valentines you can find! Jacques and Marie were nothing compared to what I could give you!"

"Get out! Just get out!" He strode to the door and flung it open. A crystal chandelier in the hall shed rainbow refractions on his arms. Broken light.

Perry hung back. "This is the only way I can get what I need. You can't throw me out now." His drawl was almost a whine.

"I can." Malachi let go of the door and reached out, grabbing Perry's left arm. "And I will."

Perry jerked away from him. "But I'm not even dressed!"

Malachi grabbed him harder, pulling him close. "Then get dressed!" he said, yanking them face to face, twisting the arm. "And then get out!"

The closeness was unexpectedly intimate. Malachi could feel Perry's breath on his face, hot honey, spice, a little

of the outside rain. Then Perry smiled. "Okay. Okay. I'll go."
And Malachi's hands dropped like weights to his sides. All
energy left him. That damned smile. The softened voice. His
hunger was drawn to it, as if it might feed off those small but
calculated gestures.

Perry blinked, lips still haunted by that smile, turned
away and went into the bedroom. Malachi felt the pull again.

Pain angled through him. It tasted of rejection, and a
spoiled boy's frivolous ideas dashed for the night. He'd get
over it. But the lingering essence of Perry had spoiled the
evening completely. All Malachi wanted to do now was sleep.

A stale bitterness pushed at his skin, his mind. He
paced the room again, pausing over the soft white light bulbs
in a pair of matching lamps on a long table along one wall. He
needed more light. He really should go back to Tania where
he was comfortable and in control. But he was not yet ready.

Finally, he lay back on the couch and closed his eyes.
He did not realize how drained he was. Sleep threatened him
as if it knew this was his last escape from the storm, his
famine, the night.

It was still night when he startled awake. At first he
thought he was chasing a nightmare. Then, with a surge of
anger, he remembered Perry. He remembered lying on the
couch. But that was all.

He couldn't see. The room chilled through him. His
body felt mushy, almost paralyzed. Though he still felt he was
in his hotel suite, the taste of the room had changed to one of
bile, despair, the tears of soured souls.

Immediately, he tried to sit up, but found he could not.
Something metal held his hands together over his abdomen.
Something else had caught at his ankles. How could he have
slept through being bound like this? What had Perry done?

He bent his knees, trying to lift himself up again.
"Perry!" he called, anger tearing through him like acid. His

60

voice sounded off, disposable, tight with a weakness he tried to deny.

"I'm right here. Can't you see me?"

"Perry!" Now his voice dropped. He took a deep breath for power, only to experience dizziness. "Turn on the light."

"You want the light? But it weakens you so. Don't you understand? It's not the dark that's been draining you all these years."

"And so to prove it you've tied me up?" he growled. He felt like the loser in a kid's game of heroes and villains.

"To prove you wrong. You need the light and you need love. So you say. To live forever. But what happens if you don't get it? Do you die then? I don't think so. But I want to know for myself, and since you'll tell me nothing…"

Malachi concentrated on breathing. The dark became a stench, and he could smell every molecule of its essence, every grief that shuddered it, every flame it murdered. It was like being buried in brackish water, the froth and mire choking him with muddied ash and dust and rot.

That Perry would do this to him! It was outrageous. Yes, the kid was certainly capable of deviousness, but this?

"Maybe," said Perry's voice in the dark, "if you tell me what I want to know, if you give me what I want, I'll think about letting you go."

Malachi did not reply. His eyes were adjusting to the terrible blackness. He could see now that the curtains on the windows were open. Lights from the still-awake city drifted in on the shadows left by raindrops slipping down the glass. Malachi tried to concentrate on that very little bit of light, go into it, expand upon it. It took all his energy, and even then he could drink and taste only the tiniest portion of hope. Lodged here and there were the seeds of it, but love—he had already forgotten that nectar.

Marie and Jacques: What had they looked like? Did she have blonde hair, or brown? Was he the taller? Did his eyes reflect the sky? And the couple before them, grown old and tired in their lives, but never in their love. What had that been like? The thrill of being in love for fifty years without respite, the ecstasy of passion and support and praise. It was as if his memory could no longer contain this knowledge, the flavors of his cravings, the so-necessary essence of how Malachi had chosen to be.

Perry interrupted the silence again, impatient as he always had been as a teenager. "Tell me the truth, and maybe I'll turn on the lights."

"Let me go first." It was a weak plea. Inside him forces were warring. Perry's voice and intentions and spirit were condemning him.

"You're in no position to give orders anymore. I want what you have. And you won't help me. Now I can force you. Do you understand?"

The sun will come up, Malachi told himself. The dawn and the lovers will mingle.

"Why don't you tell me?"

"Because I don't know." He squirmed.

"Bullshit!" The word, in English, sounded perfectly Austrian. Malachi almost laughed.

"You are wrong," Malachi began, his voice hoarse, grating.

"I don't believe you. You know things. And you keep them from me. I'll kill you if I have to! I swear it!"

Malachi shut his eyes, his throat thickening. "No," he said.

"No?"

Suddenly, a hand was at Malachi's throat. He felt something sharp there, pricking the skin like a cold edge of ice. He couldn't move. If he did, the ice would go into him. He dreaded the final result. But maybe it wasn't too late.

"Perry, don't—"

"Like I said, you're in no position to give orders!"

"I'm in no position to give you what you want, either," he rasped. A wind thrummed with a burst of hard rain against the window behind him. The room seemed to move as the dripping shadows rode the far-off, outside lights. He thought he could hear the sea now, foam cantering on the backs of waves. *Something lost; something gained.* That was what the sea said every time it touched the shore with a grain of sand, then took another into its embrace.

"Perry, you must stop. Please." He gave it one last try. "It's you who are behaving against your nature. You could have been what I wanted if you had just tried."

"I am already what you want!"

"You think so?"

"I know so! But you keep shoving me aside." On the last words, the boy's voice dropped. Malachi thought he heard a stifled sob. Then the sharpness at his neck pushed in.

Ice. Zing of pain. Sorrow. Ruin. Drought.

He felt the blood spurt as he came up, fast, off the couch. Whatever had bound his ankles shredded as he kicked. The handcuffs around his wrists shattered.

Perry screamed. Malachi could see him now, clearly, as Perry's intentions reflected into him and became him. As Perry's fears and resentments, the pain of a child who'd lost his parents, the pain of never being accepted by others became his, ripping through him, filling all the blank places where the cells yearned for the memory of love, but could not find it.

In one last effort, Malachi put his arms around the boy, seeking light, seeking anything that would counteract these opposite effects. He wanted to believe Perry had something of value buried deep, hidden, afraid to be seen. Please, he silently begged, give me any shred of decency. Compassion. Fascination. Beauty beyond the skin. Beyond the hair and eyes that could have, if he'd made it to L.A., sold them all in Hollywood to tomorrow's new star.

But there was nothing except Perry's lust for Malachi, for his "forever". And now, there was his fear.

A distant memory came to him. A dark street in an ancient, long dead part of the world. A homeless boy weeping from the cold. How Malachi had fed and fed on that. Distilled tears. Hatred for anything that wasn't of this harsh perfume.

Malachi's hunger attached itself to those repulsive sensations again, forced now by the denial of light to take this in, to sustain itself on what Perry could give.

Selfishness. Dishonor. False souls. The bitters of Perry made a dark liqueur.

Perry squirmed and moaned. Yelled and wept.

Malachi held him tighter, reverently but without love, until the boy quieted.

After he was finished soaking the despair of Perry into him, he let him down to the soft carpet with a gentleness he did not feel. He swept his hand down the beautiful body, the chest hard and pulsing with hated mortality, the stomach quivered by fear, the full genitals thrust toward him as if to say, *I demand you*. Malachi cupped them in his palm through the tight Spandex of the boy's shorts, then moved down to touch the muscled thighs, hard knees, backing away from him as he reached Perry's feet.

The boy lay, withered by tears and hatred. He breathed hard, as though he were ill.

Malachi knew, as he had always known with his lovers, that the intensity would pass, the illness recede. Perry would live. But without pleasure. And because of the boy's foolishness, Malachi would live, too, his deeper nature reawakened, compelled now to seek out darkness and disgrace, terror in the cracks of night's suffocating face, disease that opposed every aspect of the day, until a time when someone, enemy or friend, might once more shackle him, starve him, and return him to the light.

Hello Darkness

When I go to him it is by invitation only, hand-delivered. The paper of the invitation is thick, always blue. The writing is precise, flowing. Polite. My name is hand-printed on the envelope in sprawling letters: **Griffin.** He never calls me Fin as all my friends do.

The instructions on the invitation always include a date, a time. The address I know by heart. Our ritual has been a weekly one for six months. I know exactly where to go.

The house sits back from a road with only one street-light. Tree-shaded. At night the shadows are so dark they are blue. I let myself into the backyard by the side gate where azaleas and trumpet vines sweeten the air. By starlight I can make out their blooms, fluorescent pinks, translucent golds. The brick path takes me to a pair of French doors. Always unlocked.

I enter at the appointed time.

A sunroom in no sun.

Walls that seem to lean because soft tapestries I can barely see in the dimness adorn them ceiling to floor.

A cozy thrill. An odd warmth.

When I first came to this place my fear almost made me run. It seemed a trap. The well-made nest of an unknowable being who refused light of any kind.

But the kindness of the voice when he introduced himself, the gentle instructions, calmed me.

I part heavy curtains, velvet against my palms, smelling of musk and wine and desperate wishes.

A quickening of flame that reveals nothing but a blue pucker on the air...

My first time I thought it was a cigarette. But he does not smoke. The match is put to incense, more woodsy aromas to confuse me, assault my senses.

The ritual varies little week to week.

Hello darkness, my old friend.

Hello to craving and secrets and enigma.

Hello to the soft low voice that instructs me.

"Please remove all your clothes, Griffin, and place them on the bench you will feel to your left."

Standing in such blindness, waiting naked is a more vulnerable state of being than I have ever known. And for this moment every week, for six months, I've kept my body hair shaved. I've grown to love it.

People believe light exposes them, all their traits, their little faults, wrinkles, freckles, dimples, tangles. But it is darkness which exposes us for who we truly are.

Here in this house on the edge of perpetual night I am suddenly without identity for these moments, my body seeming to expand to seek out the space, explore it with all my other senses.

I can hear him breathing, steady, even. My skin feels the heat of it; the spiced perfume of him effusing my skin. I taste the humid, incense smoke.

"Griffin, walk two steps forward," he commands.

I obey. Months ago I agreed to the ritual. I always do as he says.

I sense him moving.

He circles me twice. Always twice. I hear the air pass through his nostrils as he takes me in, my own scent, my uniqueness. It must be good for him. His sighs are thin but carry amplified excitation through the dark.

Never has he touched me with his hands. I long for it. But I can only dream of that day. Hands are not his preference. Touching is achieved in another manner.

The first time, before I knew how he behaved, he had to gently reassure me. "Do not be afraid. I will never hurt you."

Now I stand still, body tingling in yearning, skin flushed.

Sometimes he begins at the back of my leg. Sometimes at the neck. Or shoulder blade. Twice at the thigh. A dozen times at the small of my back.

Tonight he chooses the ribbed skin just below my left nipple.

Short, quick, rough licks. Very cat-like. Wet and warm.

His hair is long. I know that much. As his quick tongue bathes my skin the edge of the soft cool fringe brushes my hip.

When he starts at a mid-point on my body I never know if he'll continue the bath up or down.

Tonight he goes up. I cannot suppress a shiver as his tongue laps a complete path over and around my nipple.

I have been aroused since I walked past the curtains, since before I removed the first article of my clothing.

There is nothing I can do about that. Absolutely nothing.

He licks a line to my neck, curls his tongue over my left ear, outlining it. Where he touches, my skin flames. He moves to my jaw. My cheek. My lips. His licks are like a kiss. The sweetest kiss. I want more but when I move my head slightly forward the tongue draws back, giving only light, feathery flicks.

I hold myself as still as possible. He rewards my cooperation with more fervent lapping, tongue parting my lips, stealing inside. Firm. Tasting of caves and deepness and a little of the sea. His lips finally brush mine, sending darts of pleasure through my chest, my abdomen. Too soon he moves away.

He laves my chin, my right shoulder, browsing his way down the arm. When he gets to my hands he takes his time with each finger. Pinky first. Ring. Middle. He tongues the delicate webbing between them, then gently sucks each one deeply into his hot mouth. The thumb is last. I press it against his tongue and he suckles it harder. He pulls off and leaves little wet lines on my palm that cause shivers up both arms all the way to my nape.

From my palm at rest by my hip he makes the leap to new flesh, slowly drenching my hipbone, the outer thigh, the side of one buttock with his thin and easy moisture, licking, grazing, dining.

Where the gentle curve of skin meets the back of my thigh, he delves, patiently making his way along the gentle crevice to where the muscles curve inward. The tongue extends, traveling diligently and thoroughly up the crack of my ass. He does not require me to bend or move. He simply presses inward. His lips and mouth caress as his tongue artfully rims me.

It is not hot or cold in this room, but sweat beads in my hair.

My whole body is flame now. Surely I must glow in the dark.

The press of that wet muscle against such a sensitive area along with deprivation of sight makes me dizzy. He seems to sense when I am losing control, has perfect timing in that way. He finishes with a plush tongue-swirl at my tailbone and moves along.

Down one leg, behind the knee. A seeping warmth laps at my ankle, my foot, the webs of my toes.

Another leap, this time from foot to foot as my other toes are laved, taken, swallowed.

Then up he goes on the other leg, taking the most time to cover and wash the inside of the back of my knee.

He moves slowly up one thigh, dousing the inside until it is dripping, then on to the other thigh, sucking softly at the tender skin, tasting me until I am reduced to tremors.

My erection is so taut that even standing, gravity cannot keep it from curving up toward my belly. He has easy access to my balls and spends a lot of time there grazing, sipping, washing. Sometimes it is so intense I think my mind will split. The way he worships me. The way he tastes and tickles and devours, it is as if I am a sumptuous meal and he a man trapped too long in some desert isolation. And yet he does not gulp. I am like a delicacy. He takes his time. Enjoys.

I am ready to explode but he holds back. With light, deft laps he laves the entire length of my shaft, just tongue and dampness up, down, under, over. The licking circles the head, swift, light. The organ bobs. This does not disturb his pace, his perfection. His tongue naturally follows every twitch and throb, never leaving it alone for a moment, always in contact, always caressing.

Sometimes I can't hold back. The silence of the room and of him can be intimidating. But heavy sighs escape me, sometimes moans and growls. I have no control anymore. It is given all to him.

I cannot think in more than abstract color; sensate pleasure engulfs me as my eyes squint shut.

My mind tumbles, soars. It beats at its cage of flesh and time. The nova is in me. Pure expansion. Glittering ecstasy.

As his mouth welcomes me I am instantly taken to other realms, my entire body pulsing in orgasm. I am slipping and sliding on waves of stars. There are revelations I have only begun to explore. A part of me so long submerged from the world of daylight and responsibility and manners surfaces, gasping. The curtain is pulled back on another self, primal, true, real.

I long to know who is doing this to me, and why. This isn't my normal behavior, or anything to do with my normal life. No money is exchanged. This mystery man found me through a friend and the invitation was sent with the expectation of a night of pleasure with no strings attached. I almost threw it away.

For six months I have lived for this one night a week, all my days comprised of waiting no matter what I am doing, anticipating this meeting, this beautiful moment with him.

I want to hold him, touch him, see him. But I am afraid. We both are. What we can imagine and dream in the dark empowers us. Blind to visual identity and expectation, we can be more than just the shell of every role we've ever played in ordinary life.

After I am spent, the tongue cleanses, his breath exults me. The dark blazes, black on black.

I leave his house radiant, transcended. Everything is fragrant, mouth-watering, the whole world a nectar to imbibe. Passion is everywhere. Fevers. Appetites. All because of my mystery man.

As I pull away from the curb in my car, my eyes look gold in the rearview mirror. Unearthly. Nothing else is real anymore.

This moment, this feeling…I must make it last for six days until again the invitation to darkness comes. And I accept.

The Vampire's Advice

The vampire lived in a mooncast shadow just beyond the ordinary dreams that littered the streets.

He had a coat of black feathers.

He had hair the color of boiled bronze.

He had the vision of hyper-space oracles.

Most humans could not perceive him. Most animals could.

The humans who could see him came to him with questions, and for advice.

One evening, when the moonlight thickened in the lanes and the stars swayed beyond the edge of the void, a boy approached, tall and long-limbed, with dark hair swinging in his eyes. He said, "There is so much pain in this world. I want to know only of happiness and love."

The vampire said, "Happiness is fleeting. It cannot be contained. Love includes sorrow and pain."

The boy went away, discontented.

Another evening when the wind brushed its scent of scarlet leaves into the damp-bright gutters, a girl came to the vampire and asked, "When I have the child that grows now within me, how can I leash him to me forever?"

The vampire raised his head and his golden eyes saw right through her. He replied, "We are, all of us, unique and truly alone. Even if you lived forever with a caged child, you would come to realize loneliness never left you, and that you had raised another to know only limited growth and ultimate despair."

The girl left, discontented.

Later, an owl flew down and landed on the vampire's left shoulder. For hours it sat, silent and content.

The vampire smiled, reached up and fastened a thin, silver chain about the owl's leg.

The owl cocked its soft head and blinked. "This, after what you just told that girl? Even if I flew away, I would come back. I always do, don't I?"

The vampire replied, "So far, my stygian friend. But despite the advice I have given to others, I am not whole enough, nor wise, to set you free and be sure."

Fall in Love with Your Demon

Before you fall in love with your demon, you must first learn to love thorns, ruins, spinach, spiders.

The things you were taught to scorn must be again examined.

Re-learn to love the rain, sleeplessness, feral dogs.

The math you failed in school.

Poetry.

Tests.

Taking out the trash.

Sometimes the world shifts to mindless, numb eras. The humans excel at war. Politics. Hate.

Re-learn to love all people anyway, as you would a child still evolving, growing emotional skill.

Learn to love the mist when it blocks your way. The rock in your shoe. The crack in your bell.

Sixteen billion years have come and gone to rest upon this moment.

Your demon is the one who can teach you the most.

Ambrosia

(This story was published under the pen-name Natasha Solten, specifically written for the 1990's intensely erotic magazine "Blood Lust" and later republished in the erotic vampire zine "Prisoners of the Night".)

As Jesse walked the cold, pre-winter night, a usual routine that took hours, he observed and catalogued the world around him, making it real, pretending he could actually be a part of it. The taxis lining the streets were his ever-roving eyes, silent avenues guarded by single family homes and elm trees defined his false façade, for he looked human, in fact had once been human, but not anymore.

For Jesse, the changes within him had been less difficult to assimilate than for most vampires. To be an outcast had been normal for him, to skirt the night, to edge the stiff frontiers of societies lost to their own hearts. In addition, being gay had prepared him well, for his new life insisted he remain somewhat sequestered, and it did not bother him that his kind lived on the foundations of ill-gotten reputations. He was used to being misunderstood, and his vampire nature now merely enhanced that, while giving him the power to have whatever he wanted.

Other of his vampire acquaintances did not handle the job as well.

Tonight, deep in the city, Jesse knew, the vampire Indigo was boarding up his apartment, blackening the windows, making himself a prison he could never leave. Indigo had wanted to die from the first day he'd been made, three hundred years ago, yet could not. Soon he would become the skeletal phantom he revered—everything but the scythe—alone, insane. What Jesse tried to tell him was that their condition could not be eradicated, validated or embraced. It just was. You chose your various levels of suffering.

So Indigo decided self-sacrifice would lead to death-like enlightenment and had chosen the lowest level of suffering below, even, the reveling of worms.

In another part of the city, the stolid and stunning Fairis was living a portion of her vampire life pretending to be a normal woman. She lived with a mortal husband on one of those elm-shrouded streets of Jesse's false mask, and secretly left the house once a week to feed behind her husband's back. She was unsatisfied with her life, and yet she wouldn't leave it. There were no children in the marriage, no real promises, but she had it in her head that if she played the game it would, one day, become real. She could have the family by the fireplace playing Scrabble on cold November nights, or barbecuing the summers away while the kids she vowed to adopt ran through rainbowed sprinklers, and it would be real, and then she would know love despite, in deference to, and instead of her penchant for blood. But she hadn't even found *that* as a mortal.

Others of Jesse's kind played the role to the hilt, living in coffins or caves, leading the Hollywood pack addicted to praise and the Narcissistic existence of mirrors and fake suns. It was funny how they tried to recapture the day, how they failed to see the beauty in the night that Jesse had always known, how they convinced themselves they were just like anyone else. But the daylight existence always eventually robbed them of their beauty, made them sickly and abnormal vampires who later turned their backs on eternity and blew off their heads with ingeniously rigged shotguns.

Jesse decided it was worse if you thought what you had lost had ever been real. Jesse stayed sane because he knew otherwise. It was love that had destroyed them all. The fantasy of it, the desperate need of the only thing they knew could fill their empty lives. But for Jesse, there was no such thing as love. He'd never encountered it, therefore it did not exist. If that was a flaw, it was his only one. And it saved him.

Footsteps on an empty street distracted him from his philosophies. He looked up, his sight carving the night with red, incandescent light that made everything detailed and clear.

Eyes narrowing with effort, Jesse saw a man running, half a block away, past Collier Street. The man moved with an almost supernatural speed. At first he thought he was another vampire. "Hey!" he called and his voice cracked like the ice in the trees.

There was no response as the man kept going, loping with the grace of a tall gazelle, his long hair streaming red-gold flame. In the freezing weather, Jesse could see he wore only jeans and a UCLA sweatshirt. White tennis shoes with wings on the sides covered his feet.

Jesse jogged after him and called out again, like an owl, the vampire's greeting. "Who?"

At the sound of Jesse's voice the man skidded, turned. Their eyes met, Jesse's black to the other's fawn-colored. The man was lean, tall, and his hair waved behind him like a forbidden sun. His face was smooth as chiseled marble, pale in starlight. Something unfamiliar seemed to move beneath the skin of this person, a light, an alien essence which had donned the attire of a human body to ride the night. No, this was not a vampire…something else. Jesse's instinct told him: Not mortal, but what?

The man, now only about fifty feet away, began to laugh. "Who!" he called back, laughing harder, turning away suddenly, resuming his lope.

Intrigued, Jesse followed him, the air battering his face with delicious cold as he ran. The stranger moved from streetlight to streetlight, a graceful shadow topped with fire, his footsteps on the sidewalk soft as a heartbeat. Every few seconds, the laughter rang out, not crazed but intelligent, full of secrets.

He led Jesse on a twisting path down blocks of ruined apartment buildings, past warehouses, through a deserted, leaf-littered park. The stars overhead, usually dimmed by city lights, were thick and eerie, big as diamonds waiting to be filched. They were the only suns vampires truly loved, and yet the thing before him, now glowing reddish and gold like another kind of sun he hated, who continued to laugh as Jesse moved behind him, drew him harder than stars ever had.

They ended up scaling a fence in an enclosed community of mansions surrounding a withered winter golf course, acres of tennis courts, and an Olympic-sized, frozen black pond.

As they passed the large houses, Jesse could feel many occupants within reading, sleeping, making love. As always, an abnormal number of them were hypnotized by television, their minds shushing against the waves of darkness of the night their porch lights kept at bay. With his supernatural powers, Jesse might enter any home, stand unseen in a corner or a shadow, watch the people dream or doze or fuck. He might partake of them without them ever remembering, his teeth making little pricks in the skin that healed as he licked the blood away. He might stroke a forlorn young man to erection, drinking the issue from that as well, or push into the willing flesh of a yuppie divorcee who thought he was dreaming himself a woman only to find his nightlover a beautiful man who warmed his insides with passion as no woman ever had.

His vampire hunger opened inside him like a mouth, deep, endless. What drove him out every night, what could not be denied, was like an infectious loneliness that should have been, by right, owned only by stars and howling winter winds and buried cities that rose up like ghosts to shimmer at every dark of the moon.

But tonight, Jesse left all these potential victims behind as he rushed toward long-haired laughter.

Stopping at one of the largest houses on a hill, the strange man walked slowly, deliberately up the pathway to a huge, double door made of carved wood and bejeweled with a bronze knocker in the shape of a gargoyle's head. He opened the doors, entered, then closed them tight and hard behind him, leaving Jesse staring from the clean, new street. The three-story monstrosity was painted white with brick red trim. Two balconies jutted from the second story, one on the front of the house, one at the side. At the side balcony, a light came on, beaming from a window and drawing Jesse's will. He moved to gaze up at the window and saw, beyond drawn, sheer white curtains, a shadow move.

With the grace of a breeze, Jesse floated up to the balcony, landed on the wood-slatted flooring, and parted the curtains with a thought.

Inside, the man who was not a man or vampire, was bent over a table, his long hair flickering with the sparks of flame. When he moved back, Jesse could see he'd lit three votive candles, white, and the room seemed to glow from the tips of those bluish tongues.

Indigo, he thought, would appreciate this; the older romantic vampire had always been put off by electric lights.

Now the stranger turned, as if he'd known Jesse had been all along at the window, put out his hand and beckoned.

The myth that he needed an invitation to enter a house was just that, a myth, but this invitation was more than mere permission, more than a recognition of potential pleasure hiding in three a.m. dolor. This man had led him here. Now, as Jesse watched, he went to a large, king-sized bed at the far wall and began tossing black and red throw-pillows onto the carpeted floor. Carefully, he turned down the covers revealing snowy sheets, then faced Jesse beyond the window.

For a moment, he couldn't breathe. What was this? A trap? A joke? Jesse was the one who seduced. Jesse was the one who drew his victims to him like gravity, or who surprise them in their sleeping beds when they thought they were safest, when their masculine facades were dropped and they all, even the oldest, became boys again dreaming of summer and puppies and tree houses and rain.

Yet, he felt compelled. His hesitation drained. His caution dimmed. His mind felt for the window's lock and telekinetic energy manipulated the catch, opening it. The window slid silently on metal and plastic runners. The sheer curtains lifted like bodiless ghosts, and Jesse stepped into the room.

"Who?" The question came again from his lips before he could stop it.

The man by the bed smiled, teeth showing white and strong. "Ah," he said, his voice a rush of brook-water, "but it is *you* who called me."

Jesse shook his head, confused. This was not a victim. This was not a situation where he felt in control. "You led me here."

"Of course." His long hands touched the bed sheet, pressing the white of it against his palm. "And now we can pursue your needs."

"What--?"

Before he could get out another word, the long-haired man shook his head, laughing. "Just come here."

Jesse could not resist. It wasn't just the sight of the man—tall, self-assured, face squared with the characteristic of infinite knowledge—but the scent, too, of sweet blood like no other, of energy running through veins that could have been conduits to time itself. He could sense this, taste it in the air around the man, hear the thrum of an otherworldly pulse that promised a night of pleasure like no other. That promised more than longing, than the desperation of two who could never be one.

He approached, thinking he would have to make the first move, as always, but instead the man reached out and took him into his arms, the heat between them igniting instantly, the other's lips suddenly squeezed against his own.

His teeth began, immediately, to grow, as did his cock, pressed tight to the stranger's own crotch. A hot tongue licked at his lips and he opened his mouth to receive it.

It seemed there should have been more preliminaries. It seemed they should have at least, perhaps, exchanged names. And yet, Jesse knew instinctively that wasn't what he was here for, that wasn't what he was supposed to learn.

His lover's fingers mapped tangled roads through his hair, palms holding his head as the tongue delved deeper into his mouth. That tongue searched his teeth, teasing them, bringing them to vampire points as if deliberately enticing that part of him into being, asking to be bitten.

His cock pressed tighter against his jeans. His own hands roamed the back of his lover, moving low to cup firm, rounded buttocks. The stranger moved his body back and forth now, even as his mouth seared, thrusting against Jesse.

Finally, he pulled back. Jesse felt his breath come in spurts, his lungs aching. He made a grab for the stranger, his mental forces coming to play as he commanded: *Be still. Undo your shirt. Tilt your head back.*

But the stranger only laughed, his mind immune to Jesse's mind-talents.

"But I need…" *Blood.* Jesse felt himself ache with sudden betrayal, a pain that brought tears to his eyes.

"Oh, you can have it all, little vampire," came the water-rushed voice, "but on my terms. Your tricks won't work here unless I will them to."

Stunned, he couldn't move or think for a moment. What was this guy?

The man laughed again, then grabbed Jesse's shirt, a thick velvet button-up that Indigo had given him from his old-world treasures, and ripped it, buttons popping, from his shoulders and arms. He gasped as hot hands pressed his chest, rubbing hard against his nipples. The hands moved up and down, almost chafing him, his ribs heaving under the pressure. Was this man going to hurt him? The hands felt strong enough to crush, to mangle.

Then the hands fell to his waist, holding him tight, still, and the stranger's head fell toward him. Lips nipped and nuzzled at his pecks, sucking hard on the small, flat buds which puckered at the onslaught. His cock throbbed in empathy, thickening, lengthening even more in its tight jeans prison.

Jesse could only grip the man's shoulders and hold on. When his knees threatened to collapse, it was as if the stranger knew it before it would happen. The powerful hands at his waist guided him down to the edge of the bed, and Jesse fell back as the stranger's body covered him.

Soft sheets cushioned his back. The man's hair fell about him, tickling his neck and shoulders, tickling his arms as the mouth moved lower, sucking, kissing at his ribs, then his stomach.

Jesse's teeth were hot, sharp pokers in his gums. They were like little mouths of their own, demanding, suckling at his saliva which thickened as his arousal grew.

The heat of the stranger's mouth left burns everywhere he kissed. Jesse groaned aloud.

When the man moved away from him, hands pulling at Jesse's waistband, opening the jeans and pulling them with one, hard yank to his thighs, Jesse cried out. He felt his cock spring free, his balls stir as cool, November air hit his bare flesh. With patient strength, the stranger pulled Jesse's jeans lower, then knelt and pulled off his boots before yanking the jeans all the way off.

For a moment after he was completely nude, there was no contact between them. Only the air circled them, touching flushed skin, tingling at the moisture that had begun to seep at the end of Jesse's cock.

He was amazed he'd become aroused so blatantly, so quickly. As a vampire, he was used to responding only when he fed, only after his victim was completely under his control.

Now he felt on the verge of orgasm, and the feeding process had not even begun.

The stranger's long hair wafted against his knees and thighs, shimmering. It felt cool, soft as silk. He was panting and Jesse could feel the breath on his skin, on his throbbing cock.

"Look at you," the man said softly, tone almost accusing.

Jesse's head lifted form the sheets and he could see, where the man knelt between his legs at the edge of the bed, his belly was heaving, and his cock, without aid, stood straight up from its thatch of dark curls, quivering. His whole body felt hard, all his muscles readied, tensed in intuitive response to inevitable pleasure. His fingers gripped the loose bedspread that wrinkled just below his hips, and air passed through his erect, pointed teeth with a hiss.

"You're quite lovely," the stranger said, and Jesse saw the thick lips smile again, heard on a soft, telepathic wave more laughter.

Jesse tried to use his mind talents against him to control the guy. *Come to me. Bare your veins. Give yourself.*

The man only shook his head, smile widening. "I know what you really want."

"Please," Jesse said, trying not to beg. He could already imagine the taste of the other's blood on his tongue. It would be rich, thick, tart. It would fill him with the juice of forever, with beauty, with lust.

"So impatient," the man said. Then his head bowed. The long hair flicked at Jesse's calves. A wet mouth moved along his thigh. He thought he would die at the sensitivity of his skin, at the thrill that coursed through him from that intimate kiss.

He felt his balls tighten as the mouth moved up his thigh, could feel his lover's breath on them, and on the crease where thigh and buttock met. Without thinking, he spread his legs, lifted himself. He wanted to feel this man's kisses everywhere.

Hot breath warmed the crease of his ass beneath his balls. Then, with steady strokes, the tongue began laving the underside of his testicles. A flush of warmth flooded up his stomach, and into his cock. He thought he was going to come…but not yet.

The tongue explored him fully, tickling at the fold of skin between his balls, making circles around the small globes. Then, when he was very wet, the mouth opened. He could feel the lips caress him; the tongue licked as the mouth sucked first the left testicle, then the right, into its roiling warmth. The mouth pulled at his balls, warm, hot, and he groaned aloud, feeling his teeth ache as they tried to extend beyond their limits. His cock throbbed hotly at being ignored.

Jesse could not help it. His hips bucked in the pleasure that this man was inflicting. Mouth open, wet with the saliva that was produced when his teeth extended, he put one hand to his lips and bit down hard on the fleshy part of his palm. His own salty blood burst into his mouth, and the pain made him dizzy, crazy, even more aroused than possible at the same time.

With his free hand, Jesse reached out and grabbed his own hard cock, pulling at the stretched flesh in desperation.

The stranger backed off his balls with a smacking sound, grinning. "Oh no!" He caught Jesse's hand, holding it tightly in his own as Jesse stared at him, still feeding on his own palm.

His cock ached. He wanted to touch it again. He wanted to come. But the stranger wouldn't let him.

Back the man went to his balls. The suckling there grew stronger, and Jesse shook, straining for more, his ass tightening, clenching.

The guy moved away again, pushing Jesse's legs further apart. Jesse bent them at the knees, took his hand away from his mouth, still bloody, and pulled his knees toward him.

Immediately, he felt the mouth on his ass, biting playfully at first, then tongue delving into the crack, touching lightly at his asshole.

The room spun. Jesse needed to drink, his hunger churning, yet he didn't want the pleasure to end so he did not move.

The deep kissing sounds increased. He felt his asshole penetrated by both a finger and a tongue, and wiggled to show he craved more.

"Ah," the man said. "Yes."

But instead of continuing, he moved away from Jesse again, rising up to stand over him. He reached out to touch Jesse's hairless chest, fingers pressing at the nipples, then stroking lower to the belly and circling, but not touching, the erect and trembling penis.

"Christ!" Jesse screamed. His teeth were like knives pressing his lips.

"Not quite," the man replied, chuckling. He continued to stroke Jesse's hips, his smiling eyes watching as Jesse's hard cock swayed and shivered.

Finally, the guy grabbed the base of his cock and held it still, not stroking, just holding. Jesse's breath caught. The pressure of the fingers at the base held him at bay and slowly, as he watched, the stranger bent, kneeling again between his legs, and lowered his mouth to the tip of his cock. First, just the lips touched him, a light kiss on the glans. The mouth glistened with Jesse's pre-cum as he pulled back, and a tongue snaked out and licked the moisture away, then licked curiously at the tip of his cock.

Something inside him shriveled at the touch. Something else grew. Something like flame deep inside where the vampire hunger that was empty-Jesse existed, where all his fears and disbeliefs lived, where self-doubt and alienation vied for supremacy.

84

As he felt himself open as he had never been before, his aching teeth drew back, still sharp, still hungry, but hesitant now, curious.

The tongue massaged him gently at first, then harder, curling against the ridge of his penis, exploring under and over, before, finally, the lips touched him, surrounded him, pulled him into the most luscious, hot mouth he'd ever experienced.

The head of his cock expanded—at least that's how it felt to Jesse—as the guy sucked it. The hand at the base of his cock moved, but very slowly, gently. Several times, the guy pulled back a little, letting the wet head of his cock pop from his lips before inserting it into his mouth again.

Fingers touched his balls, cupped them. The mouth descended, taking more of him in, pulling up a little before pushing down another inch, then another. Now he was being absorbed into oblivion, and he suddenly forgot how to breathe, how to live, how to enclose himself in his vampire talents, his nature, and let the beautiful darkness own him.

Light spread through his mind, against his pressed shut eyelids, swirling orange and yellow and red. It burned. Everything burned. His cock was a torch, the rest of him fuel for the pyre. He'd never been so hot, or felt such pleasure that didn't involve feeding.

His teeth throbbed but the pain in them was gone. They were behaving as though they were being satiated, as though the pleasure that shot through Jesse's body was blood and memory and lust, and not this patient, thorough examination from a man whose technique in oral sex rivaled anyone he'd ever known.

Jesse's spine flowed like water; his thighs felt like blazing logs. The man between his legs sucked harder and he thought, *This is it. I'm coming.* But suddenly, the mouth pulled wetly off him. His penis, glowing wet and rosy, plopped back onto his stomach.

Now the guy, still smiling, stood again, reaching to undo his jeans. Jesse leaned up on his elbows, watching as the pants fell and the stranger's massive erection jutted upward, golden, heavy, framed in red-gold curls. Before Jesse could do or say anything, the man grabbed Jesse's thighs and pushed Jesse back on to the bed, covering him with his own hot body. Jesse felt the big cock nudge his ass, then, without preliminaries, seek the hole and push. His asshole tensed.

"Let me in," demanded the stranger. "Now."

Stars smeared his vision as he felt the big cock root into him. His breath fell from his lips in a huge groan. He could feel the other's pubic hair tickle his balls, how his asshole stretched and the muscles within gave way to accept the intruder.

As he relaxed, his cock still harder than he'd ever thought possible, the stranger pulled back and thrust into him again. The movements increased, and Jesse held onto the bed sheets to keep from sliding back.

Now the motion grew more fluid, and the laughing man, his hair falling into his face and dusting his still sweatshirt-clad chest, began to sweat. Jesse could feel the liquid dripping onto his cock, his balls. He groaned aloud again.

"Yes!" The stranger moaned in return, then reached out and grabbed Jesse's cock, pumping it in time to his thrusting. The hand was strong, but not hurtful. It stroked him from base to tip, squeezing just right, and inside the big cock found and rubbed at the most sensitive of places. His balls felt like they were bursting as the cock pinned him to the bed. The hand on his penis stroked up, down, shaking it a little, petting the tip with his strong thumb.

It was too much. Jesse thrust up, then back onto the huge, ramming cock, then up again and held utterly still. The stranger sensed his imminent release, and pushed harder with his cock, stroking Jesse's erection faster, faster.

Jesse screamed. Liquid shot from his cock in an arc, wetting his chest, his belly. The throbbing convulsions lasted longer than they ever had before as he kept coming, white strings of juice pulsing from him. At the same time, he felt the stranger tense, and warm fluid filled his insides.

Slowly, the man lowered himself to Jesse's body. His cock was still inside Jesse, and he tossed his long hair aside, exposing his throat. "Now," he said softly, pulling Jesse's head to his neck.

The teeth hungered, but sweetly now, not needy but still wanting. They dug like little pins into the offered, golden flesh, and found there an elixir like none other. Jesse drank the sweetness, hands fondling the stranger's back and ass as the guy's cock stayed hard within him.

When he pulled back, he saw the mark of his vampire nature on his lover's throat, but instead of red stains, there was gold liquid on the skin, marking the tiny holes with honeyed drops.

Dizzy with pleasure, Jesse barely noticed as the man began more thrusting, as his own cock hardened and they did it all over again.

Later, when the curtains billowed in a pre-dawn, near-freezing November breeze that neither man's heat even noticed, Jesse said, softly, again, "Who?"

"I bleed ambrosia. Don't you know?"

"God…"

"Yes. Some call me Eros. Some Cupid. I came to enter you, to be inside you forever. You called me, though you don't know it. You never believed in me. But now you have no choice. And neither one of us will ever be alone."

Again, the hard cock within him magically hardened. Jesse barely noticed the sun rising fluorescent orange through the curtains as night bled away from him to the other side of the world and he was accepted for the first time in the light, dark nature and all.

Future, Future

Blood sea future,
riptides of a past—
like the moon
you are cratered
with a dark side,
you, jumbled vampire,
stalking stars while
all those jiminy crickets
purr down
your village night.
The drylands are close,
the badlands
coming up to the door
of your infinity.
You can book passage
only on the bone trains,
only through dust alleys
where dune ships
will take you
to the land of fear,
to the melt-desert
and you will touch
the totem
that is self,
that is stone
after an eternity
of realizing you
mistakenly chose
the blood for the heart.

Husks

(for Louis)

I love the sad ones,
beings whose dreams walk the dead lamp of
the moon,
who have more than a little of the
dark mantra
in their souls.

The sad ones make autumn their flag,
cast dust-confetti,
carve out a frail and brooding existence
in window-locked houses,
collect tears like tea in cups.

I love the sad ones
bowing to their thin candles,
caping themselves in cool lengths of black,
so close to the truth of their world,
yet so far from home.

Husks

There is a solar eclipse today, and so we rise in unusual confusion while it is still afternoon. Barclay complains because his rest has been interrupted. But I, always an early-riser, fill my vision with the dusk of the streets outside the casement window, smiling at the extended moments, the little time to add more richness to my life. I imagine the prey to be different by day. Not the usual night-lovers, but those fleshy beings who hide themselves away after sunset behind glowing curtains, who give their warm wills to the flickering screens of the fantasy box.

As if merely to irritate, morose Barclay turns on the TV. "Daytime shows," he observes. "Wow." It's the most enthusiasm he's shown in weeks.

It is 1969. He sits in a crushed-velvet chair (my favorite piece of furniture left over from the last century) to watch *Let's Make a Deal.*

"Charles," he says, "we could get on this show easy. Look at those people! They're stranger than we are." He rubs his long, blond hair back from his bony forehead.

I do not look. I am the hunter. I must touch my prey. Make them feel what I feel, love what I love. The television does not allow this. And Barclay, from this newer era, has never caught on to the true nature of the wonder of what we are. Or of what it means to hunt. I love him, but I failed to give him the strength it takes to make him last. I do not know how many more days we will have together, but anything less than eternity is never enough.

"I want to go out," I say.

He turns, eyes dark with shock. "You can't. The sun will come out from behind the moon again any minute."

"I know." He's always been more concerned for my welfare than his own. "I didn't say I would."

He offers a soft smile and my blood quickens. Still, after two years, he can do this to me. I go to him. *Let's Make a Deal* is forgotten as I bend to him, my lips pressing the hotness of his sharp cheek. His lashes brush my nose.

We have maybe minutes before we will fall asleep again. The clock says 1:25 p.m. The dark is not normal. The frailness of him is more apparent than ever. The day reveals our creases, sucks the magic from us even with the sun hidden behind that dust-ball moon. It is cruel, and I see Barclay is more lost to me than I thought.

Barclay never had the blood enough to survive. I knew this when I made him, and as I now take his thin body to mine, I know it more. He is not a hunter. He was never anything but prey. And love is the betrayer whose hope leads only to gloomier domains. Yes, Barclay was dangled in my face. The gods' voices in my head said, *You can have him if you want him, but of course you can never keep him.* So I took him, little baby with his hair spread across my chest, blood thin and warm and thready in my mouth, boyish with charm but no dimension, lovely in deed but half-formed in thought.

Why do I always fall for the mannequins, the wraiths who already haunt their skeletal bodies, who will benefit none from the strength I can give?

I've tried to save him three times from the special suicides of our kind: fire, revealing yourself to the mortal public (we had to move to another city), and now self-imposed starvation.

He kisses me readily, but I know it's for my own comfort. There is no respite for him. After I fill my mouth with my own blood, taken deftly from a vein in my wrist, I kiss him harder on the lips, letting the red-salt trickle. He chokes and shudders, refusing the swallow.

The room lightens. He's still shaking as I take him back to our closed, narrow bed. By evening, it's a skeleton I hold, an old doll, a memory.

I rise, turn on the TV. "Let's make a deal!" I whisper to that devil which has enslaved the fleshier dayshine prey until only the ones like Barclay venture out at night where I will find them, where I will fall for them again and again.

Outside, the moon is still full, sinking from the stars. I fill the room with howls.

The Shadow Garden
1.

I light the tower windows
I light the black tapers
Thunder and dreams
reach me through you

*

There are wolves
in the garden
I leave the gate open

The Shadow Garden
2.

Like a sleepwalker
I go
into the moon's lullaby

*

I see only evenings ahead
thousand upon thousand
uninterrupted by the day's
unwelcome fevers

I sleep in the light
hidden and frail
touching my thighs for warmth
shallow-breathing so that
the broken hearts
of all the wakened world
cannot lodge in me

The dreams of my ghost-hood
soar like crows

I dress in black
I look into blind windows
only to see myself

The Shadow Garden
3.

You lie
in a garden
of painted mushrooms
listening to
the stories
of the green river
passing by

There are whispers of
shamans and totems,
the sunken city
of an alien prince,
quartz crystal caves
and immortal lichen,
a Spanish galleon lost
in time,
lands of ambient light,
a pale beach where
shapeshifters dance,
a red fountain
where the vampires come
to drink

The green river whispers
of worlds like marbles
flung along its shores

The Shadow Garden
4.

Already I am your child
grown thin in the light

Leaf-bred I hang
upside-down in October trees

Vampire Children

They do not shiver in snow.
They eat pepper and garlic
with radishes and mint.
They move within your eyes
like peripheral ghosts
almost cloudy, almost not there.
They do not get colds.
They cannot find clothes that fit.
Their voices are scratched gold
and autumn rust.
The sun is repelled
by their swift withdrawals.
The moon leaves traces of lavender
upon their skin and hair.
They dance with the goat-footed shadows.
Pluto is their king.

Wendy Rathbone has had dozens of stories published in anthologies such as: Hot Blood, Writers of the Future (second place,) Bending the Landscape, Mutation Nation, A Darke Phantastique, and more. Over 500 of her poems have been published in various anthologies and magazines. She won first place in the Anamnesis Press poetry chapbook contest with her book "Scrying the River Styx." Please visit her Amazon Author page for a list of all her publications.

You can visit her blog at:
http://wendyrathbone.blogspot.com/

Her recent books include:

The Moonling Prince Book 1
The Coming of the Dark: The Moonling Prince Book 2
"This Wish Tonight" Christmas Anthology (Mischief Corner Books).
Lace, book 1 in the vampire fairy series, m/m romance.
Scoundrel, science fiction m/m romance novel.
"Beneath the Blue Dusk and the Sea," short story collection.
"Turn Left at November," a brand new collection of poems.
"Letters to an Android," science fiction novel.
"Pale Zenith," science fiction novel.
"Moltenrose," two stand-alone novellas in the Pale Zenith universe.
"The Foundling," male/male romance novel, book 1 of the Foundling trilogy.
"None Can Hold the Dark," book 2 of the Foundling trilogy.
"The Lostling," book 3 of the Foundling trilogy.
"The Secret Sharer," science fiction romance novella.
"Unearthly," omnibus collection of 7 out-of-print poetry booklets.
"The Vampire Diaries: The Myth," available from Kindle Worlds.
"The Vampire Dairies: Deep in the Virginia Woods," available from Kindle Worlds.
"My House is Full of Whispers," erotica short story collection.

She lives in Yucca Valley, CA with her partner of 36 years, Della Van Hise.

Previous Publication Credits

Bitters was previously published in *Prisoners of the Night #9*. *It was republished in the DNA Publications collection* *Dream of Decadence Presents Wendy Rathbone and Tippi N. Blevins, 2002.*

The Boy Without a Soul was previously published in *Zero Gravity Freefall*. *It was reprinted in the DNA Publications collection* *Dreams of Decadence Presents Wendy Rathbone and Tippi N. Blevins, 2002.*

The Phantom on the Road was previously published in the DNA Publications collection *Dreams of Decadence Presents Wendy Rathbone and Tippi N. Blevins, 2002.*

Hello Darkness was previously published for free on the private m/m romance Goodreads group in 2014.

Husks was previously published in *Prisoners of the Night #10,* 1997.

Ambrosia was previously published in *Blood Lust* (Masquerade Publications) and reprinted under the name Natasha Solten in *Prisoners of the Night #10,* 1997.

The poems *Future, Future, Husks, The Shadow Garden 1-4, Vampire Children* were previously published in *Prisoners of the Night #8, #10* and *#11,* 1994, 1997 and 1999.

The Vampire's Advice and *Fall in Love with Your Demon* both appear here for the first time.

THE MOONLING PRINCE
Wendy Rathbone

Tahir is an empath and a healer. He has lived his whole life at the Onyx Temple. When the king from the Realm of the September Stars seeks his help, Tahir leaves his own world behind to answer the plea.

Arulu is the crown prince of the September Stars, but he cannot serve. For twenty years he has suffered crippling pain, the side-effect of a splinter-bomb attack from unknown origins that destroyed the Realm's home world, Lyric Prime.

For two decades no one has been able to ease the prince's suffering, until Tahir arrives. But nothing is ever easy. Haunted by ghosts and riddled with mistrust, Arulu is no normal patient.

Can Tahir ever hope to earn Arulu's trust?

Will Arulu survive the aftermath and grief of the healing process?

Love is the master of healing, but for Tahir and Arulu it is not an easy road.

Available on Amazon
or www.eyescrypublications.com

The Coming of the Light
Wendy Rathbone

In *The Moonling Prince: Book One,* the empath Tahir is called upon to heal Prince Arulu of the Realm of the September Stars. His mission is successful and he stays on at the King's Court as the official Palace Healer. Meanwhile, Tahir and Arulu begin to fall in love but it is no easy road as Arulu battles grief, PTSD, his twin brother's ghost, and other problems resulting from his tragic past.

The Moonling Prince: Book Two takes the reader on a deep and intimate journey into the private relationship of Ari and Tahir as they continue to get to know each other.

During the weeks-long celebration of the holiday called *The Coming of the Light,* Ari faces long days in his father's court surrounded by politics and begins to question his destiny as future king of the Realm.

Tahir must battle his own feelings of alienation and loneliness in a realm and culture he was not raised in, as well as bigotry and threats from visiting delegates of the court.

Meanwhile, the king is planning a momentous change for the entire conglomerate of moons.

Can Ari and Tahir's new bond survive a meddling king and father, threats to Tahir's life, and Ari's own hidden darkness? Can love conquer grief as well as cultural rifts? All leads to an explosive conclusion on a moon called Firgone in a realm known as the September Stars.

Available on Amazon or
www.eyescrypublications.com

Turn Left at November

**Poems by
Wendy Rathbone**

Visit realms of diamond rain, dust-folk lands and valleys of curses and shame. Reside in the burning moonships of dream, the silt of stars, the asphyxiation of the waking day. Meet the golden android who houses your soul. Journey through tatters of stardust down roads of sorrow. Find hope in planets of candles and crazy-eyed mermen. There you will meet November in these rich and evocative poems by Wendy Rathbone.

Unmaking Autumn

*Out at the excavation site
where they are taking apart autumn
leaf by fabled leaf
the searchlights try to catch us
putting the eyes back into the pumpkins
the moon back in the witch-shaped sky
We steal blood kisses
behind the naked apple orchards*

**On Amazon or from
www.eyescrypublications.com**

LETTERS TO AN ANDROID
Wendy Rathbone

Cobalt is a created human, vat grown and born adult, with no human rights and indentured to serve others for the duration of his life. Liyan is a young man with wanderlust in his eyes, embarking on a career that takes him to the furthest regions of space. The two become unlikely friends and create a memorable long-distance correspondence. Through Liyan, Cobalt gets to explore the universe, living vicariously through his friend's wave transmissions. A strong bond develops between them that not even the stars can put asunder.

———————————

Now you know an android who writes poetry.
This is all your fault. Did you not read my last wave telling you extracurricular activities for my kind are discouraged? Of course this is harmless and strangely enjoyable and does not necessarily require me to leave the hotel. Pel would not care if I wrote lines of equations or nonsensical juxtaposed words. As long as the act does not bring my mental state into question.
However, in history, poetry is often written by the rebels.
So we can keep this to ourselves.
Let me know about your lieutenant's test.
And to give you peace of mind, I never believed you observed me as anything other than human.
Some people are and always will be hateful bigots. Most people are simply uncomfortable in speaking to "property." And anyway, friendship, like poetry, is also discouraged.

Your friend,
Cobalt

FROM THE AUTHOR:
www.eyescrypublications.com

Also on Amazon

SCOUNDREL
Wendy Rathbone
A male/male romance

Antares is a willing sex slave, trained in the harems of Anada since the age of 18, and owned by a wealthy master who spoils his slaves. But all that changes when Empire soldiers invade Antares' world and he is taken away from the only life he's ever known.

In a colonized galaxy where starships are as common as houseflies, and a dark Empire seeks to control thousands of civilized worlds, there are those who fall through the cracks and refuse to be conquered, including the pirate, Slate, and his crew.

Out in the darkness of the unknown, among Empire soldiers and scoundrels, will bad fates befall Antares and his fellow captive companions?

Will Slate finally find the love he's been looking for his whole life?

Can Slate and Antares ever see eye to eye?

A male/male romance to end all male/male romances!

FROM THE AUTHOR
www.eyescrypublications.com

Also ON AMAZON

PALE ZENITH
Wendy Rathbone
A Science Fiction Novel

On a far-flung "Earth" in a parallel universe, two factions are fighting a decades-long psychic war. Young talented psychics are being temporarily kidnapped from present day Earth, seemingly at random, to serve as part of one side's psychic army. They are put under the control of spychiatrists, mysterious machines with many limbs that have a programmed ability to travel time and space and universes to kidnap and control carefully selected humans. The humans never know they are being used; when their missions are completed they are brought back to their universe through time and placed back in their beds, their memories wiped.

The shadows wound the tall corridor in muted gold, varnished brown. It seemed as though they were in the bowels of a giant serpent coiled outside time, outside space.

When they left the palace, a familiar sun flourished in a clear, blue sky. But this wasn't their sun. Not Zack's sun. It was an alien star burning within a different galaxy in an all too distant universe. Zack looked up squinting, trying to see if he could peer beyond the sky, beyond the pale of midday and into his own timespace, but there was nothing. Only sunlight. Only the thin atmosphere of an Earth not his own.

His back knotted again. Leo's presence was a gelid space inside his chest, empty. Always before he'd felt a warmth there, a sort of pressure like someone's hand pressed gently to his heart. He'd taken Leo for granted knowing, the way a shadow falls when you block the sun, that he was there around him, inside him: blood, air, salt, brain, soul. They were genetic duplicates, twins, spiritual halves. Without him, Zack knew the first icy tugs of panic.

FROM THE AUTHOR
www.eyescrypublications.com

ON AMAZON
Pale Zenith

The Foundling
by Wendy Rathbone

Diego is a powerful man with a tragic past. Out on the expansive ocean in his private yacht, he discovers a beautiful and mysterious man adrift on a raft, near death. The bond that forms between them in the aftermath of Alec's rescue is one of fierce passion, though lacking in trust. Can they make it work, or will Alec's amnesia bring forth secrets so disturbing as to tear them apart? A passionately erotic love story of desire and darkness, exquisite and explicit.

I can see his struggle between gratitude and uneasiness. He is buffeted by all things new and strange. He does not know where he is from, who he is or what happened to him. He does not know me. There has not been enough time to transition between strangers and friendship.

This isolation of his is something I can identify with, but it is also a feeling no one can help him with until or unless he gets his own life back. And his memory.

If that doesn't happen, then it will take time for him to build a new life. He is polite to me, even friendly, but even a night together during a storm with his arms wrapped tight around my waist doesn't calm the surge I see inside him, the emptiness, the loss, possibly even panic. That night may have reinforced some trust in me, but so far not enough for him to completely relax.

He seeks me out, though. That's something. He sits by me at dinner when he can have any seat of his choosing. I watch him closely when he does not realize it. At dinner the following night after we had only 'slept' together, and before we go to bed again in separate rooms, I notice everything about him, how he moves, the way the air warms when he is closer to me, the dry sheen of his lips as they part for more air when he is reacting to something, or speaking, or eating.

His hands still shake. Anyone else might not notice because he keeps them clasped into fists at his sides or, while sitting, pressed tight to his lap.

I spend another fretful night alone. I dream restlessly, wild, loud and colorful visions I cannot recall at all as soon as my eyes open. All I know is the dreams leave me unfulfilled, impatient.

Other fiction titles from Eye Scry Publications...

Prince of Umberlight
Alexis Fegan Black

"If Prince of Umberlight doesn't rattle your cage, you're more dead than the undead!" **-Night Readers**

Thorn may be an 800 year old vampire, but he does not possess the ability to create others of his kind, and so he is cursed to fall in love with mortals, only to watch them grow old and die. Torn by grief, Thorn denounces his immortality and enters into a comatose oblivion for decades. When he awakens, he is no longer in London, but finds himself in a world spun into being by his own desires - a world where Time and Death do not exist, a world where it is forever autumn, where the Parish of Shadows and the River of Stars become his home. It is in this world of Umberlight that he meets Atom - an interloper into his private sanctuary, but also an impudent imp who is destined to reveal to Thorn the three dangerous elements a vampire must possess in order to become a Creator.

The Art of Brutality.
Submission to Dark Desire.
Love.

FROM THE AUTHOR
www.eyescrypublications.com

ALSO ON AMAZON

YEAR OF THE RAM
Della Van Hise

Year of the Ram was described by one reviewer as... "A spacefaring gay romance full of love, angst, and longing."

Only after Star Commander Morgan Diego becomes an exile as a result of a Galaxy Corps political blunder does he begin to realize how much he valued the companionship of his second in command - the mysterious Lucien, an Alfarian who is more elven than human, with peculiar powers & abilities which begin to unfold as he, too, realizes what he has lost.

Separated by circumstance from his former life, Morgan is thrust into a world where he must survive by his wits. When he meets a peculiar little old man calling himself Kim Le, Morgan finds himself in a situation where he is required to master The Art - not only a form of human & extraterrestrial martial arts, but a way of living and being that will alter his life forever.

At the temple, he is introduced to his new teacher, another Alfarian who begins to steal his heart - a heart which is already promised to Lucien. Torn and conflicted, Morgan struggles with the world he left behind and the world he now inhabits.

Beginning to believe he may never again return to his ship and to the friends and loved ones he left behind, he is all the more frustrated and heartbroken when a new Master arrives at the temple: a man to whom Morgan is immediately drawn both mentally and physically, a man who is strikingly familiar... yet utterly alien.

Year of the Ram is a fully-fleshed novel, approximately 97000 words, with a focus on the love story and romance angle. Set against a science fiction milieu, it explores the infinite possibilities of the human and alien heart. Sexual content is explicit, though is not the primary focus of the novel.

For those who like a romance that forces its characters to contemplate the ecstasies AND the agonies of love... you will enjoy *Year of the Ram* immensely.

FROM THE AUTHOR
www.eyescrypublications.com

ALSO ON AMAZON

All of our titles are available directly from our website, on Amazon, or may be ordered from most booksellers. Thanks for reading us!

Eye Scry Publications
A Visionary Publishing Company
www.eyescrypublications.com

www.ingramcontent.com/pod-product-compliance
Lightning Source LLC
Chambersburg PA
CBHW020617130626
46552CB00003B/1012